THE DEVIL'S BLOOD

To Edward,

Finian Black

Best wishes,

Finian Black

Weybourne Press

This edition published by Weybourne Press 2018

Visit the author's website at www.finianblack.com
Follow the author on Twitter @finianblack
Instagram at finianblack
Email the author at finian.black@gmail.com

ISBN-13: 978-1720341390
ISBN-10: 1720341397

Cover art © 2018 Ed Bettison

FOR M & G

1

The Shard was still smoking like an abandoned factory that couldn't quite give up its reason to exist. The smoke lifted up in stinking black clouds that mingled with the February rain. The city was still and silent. Nobody was there. Survivors of the plague had better things to be doing than sightseeing.

A pigeon fluttered among the wreckage of glass and steel, hoping to find anything to eat. It hopped under one of the police barriers erected around the scene of the explosion. The bird seemed nervous. There was none of the usual strutting walk, the energetic chatter. Things were different now. Things would never be the same again.

Two figures emerged from the shadows of a side street. The taller man limped slightly. The other one moved like a prowling tiger, scanning left and right for any sign of danger. The tall man approached the pigeon. The bird, distracted by the smell of something vaguely edible, didn't react until a boot swung angrily towards it. Just in time, the pigeon was airborne in a flurry of feathers. The man cursed quietly as he continued picking his way along the shattered pavement.

'Damn them all,' John Madoc said, his voice low and gravelly. 'Damn every rotten bird that ever lived.'

Madoc stared up at the shattered skeletal remains of the Shard. His breathing was slow and regular, but the pulse at his temple betrayed the anger that seethed through him. His fists clenched and relaxed. He reached down and rubbed at his leg before moving through the gaping hole left by the explosion, more like the mouth of a skull than a doorway into an underground car park. Instead of teeth there were bent and twisted steel girders. Wisps of smoke lifted through the carpet of smashed glass. It was warm in there. Deep in the building, fires were still burning.

'Gabriel,' Madoc hissed, 'pass me the torch.'

The other man was at his side in an instant, torch held out for his boss. Madoc played the beam across the walls and up into the unreachable darkness of the space above them. The explosion had ripped through the concrete like a hurricane across a Caribbean island.

'We're going down the ramp?'

'Yes, sir. Right to the bottom.'

'Safe?'

'Yes. Nobody's been down there. No sign of police or security forces. It will just be you and me.'

It took a long time. Before, when the building was the beating heart of Madoc's empire, it would have been a two minute stroll. In the basement car park, where Madoc's collection of cars and motorbikes had once stood in perfect gleaming rows, he gasped at the destruction.

'All that money. All that technology. Gone, just like that.'

'And all those lives, sir.'

Madoc ignored his bodyguard's comment. What did he care for the men who had died down here? They knew the risks when they joined his company. They were all former special forces and he paid them well. Death was an occupational hazard.

He carried on through the devastation. Madoc didn't pause for a moment. The men would have died instantly and that was their good fortune. He thought of the low boom of the explosion that had caused this, and the air being sucked out of his lungs just as Gabriel shoved him through a fire door, saving his life. His anger grew like a painful bite, itching away at him, just out of reach.

'They did this,' he whispered. 'Those children dared to do this to me.'

It was Gabriel's turn to stay silent, and Madoc was pleased about that. The bodyguard knew when to speak and when to keep his mouth shut. Luckily for Madoc, he also had the strength and courage to pull his boss from the Thames, saving his life for a second time.

I should be dead, Madoc thought. I should be six feet under the slime, but here I am back in the Shard. I can still do this. I can...

'Which way?' he asked. 'I can't get my bearings.'

'Over there, sir.'

Madoc swung the torch beam around. A wrecked van lay on its side up against the wall of the garage.

'Are you sure?'

'The fire escape is behind that van, Mr Madoc. It's not blocked. I reached the fourth floor yesterday. I could have gone higher.'

There was a hint of frustration in Gabriel's voice. Madoc chose to ignore it. Gabriel had rescued him. He had dragged him away from the madness of the ravens and the storm. He had found somewhere for him to rest up and recover from the broken leg he had sustained when he hit the water. Madoc owed him.

'Of course, you're right. And beyond that?'

'Only one way to find out.'

'Well, let's do exactly that.'

The still healing bone in Madoc's leg burned with the effort of the climb, but Madoc kept going, one stubborn step after the other. He pushed his way into what had been the central security room. The fire damage in here was minimal. Apart from a thick layer of black smoke that covered everything, all of the equipment was untouched. Madoc hesitated in front of the banks of monitors and hard drives, not wanting to show his ignorance.

'That one, sir,' Gabriel said, pointing at a small box.

'The last two hours of CCTV?'

'Yes. Constantly updated and saved. If it's not been corrupted by the smoke and heat, I reckon it will give you what you're looking for.'

Gabriel expertly unplugged the unit and passed it to his boss. Madoc turned it over in his hands, checking for any warping or signs of damage. Satisfied, he gave it back.

'And now up.'

'Are you sure you can make it, sir? I can go myself.'

'I'll make it if I have to crawl up every step.'

That's exactly what he did for the last five floors, knees rubbing painfully against the cold concrete, sweat dripping off him every time he paused for breath. His leg throbbed as if it was trapped in a vice. At one point, where the ceiling had collapsed and the stairwell was nearly blocked, they just managed to squeeze through the tiny gap in the broken concrete. Eventually, Gabriel pushed open the door onto the top floor and they both breathed in the cool fresh air. Madoc wiped his face on his jacket. He touched the handle of the sword at his throat. The blade was still dulled with a trace of dried blood. His head was filled with dark thoughts of what he would do to Luca Broom when he next saw him.

Then, and because anger was a waste of energy, he pushed the thoughts away and focused on what he was there to do. He ignored the smoke stained walls and carpet and headed for his office. It was eerily quiet. Every day had been a constant bustle of people and noise, stories and orders, running feet and shouted instructions. Now, the Shard was just an upright corpse. Madoc stood in front of the hole that his men had cut through the security shutters. The cutting equipment lay where it had been abandoned when the gas main had exploded three hundred metres below them.

It wasn't easy bending down. Madoc's leg screamed in resistance as he crouched down and shuffled through the hole. His hands were slick with sweat and soot but he kept going. He blinked away salty droplets, cursing softly as he heaved himself upright. The office was untouched. In the dim light Madoc could easily imagine it was a normal morning, before everything had gone wrong. Any moment now, a breakfast tray would be delivered. He would sit down at his beautiful desk and flick on the screens. He would scan the headlines playing across his channels. He would phone important people and make things happen...

'I will make them pay,' he whispered, and the perfect image faded away. He limped over to the fireplace and pushed aside the cold coals. The manual switch to release the wall worked perfectly. He pushed it open with barely any effort. Inside the hidden room, the round table still hung down from its thick steel cables. Madoc's painted image seemed to tease him instead of celebrate what might have been.

He dared to look at the plinth, holding his breath, hoping that what he had always believed would be true...and it was. The spell book had found its way back, because it wasn't just a collection of magic, it *was* magic, and it still belonged to him.

'I've a chance,' he whispered, 'if I want it.'

He picked up the book. He turned it over, checking for damage, but there was none, because nothing could destroy such a thing. He flicked through its pages, pausing for the briefest moment at the spell that had failed. He moved on. So the ravens were still at the Tower. Who cared when there was another way?

He looked down at a different spell. His eyes scanned the tightly written lines, and even as he read them the madness of what he was planning suddenly overwhelmed him. His fingertips trembled. Then he thought of Luca and what that brat had done to him, and any doubt was gone in an instant. He closed the book and slipped it into his pocket.

'I'm going to use the Devil's blood,' he whispered.

2

Rain was the only thing on Luca's mind as they headed home. It seemed endless, surging out of the sky like the overflow from a broken gutter, splashing against the windscreen of the stolen car. The wipers could barely cope with the volume of water. They whirred and flapped like broken birds' wings. The noise of it was a constant drumming, eight beats to the bar, over and over again. He closed his eyes as the car bounced along. The insides of his lids sparkled with red and orange, the colours of the night. He liked the rain. It was a cocoon against everything that had happened. In the car, there was just the two of them again.

'Can I have some water, please?' his mum asked.

He cracked the seal on a new bottle. She drank it all in one go, driving steadily, eyes on the road the whole time.

'Had enough?'

'Yes, thanks.'

He studied the outline of her face. The street lights flashed over the dark smudges under her eyes. She was still painfully thin, even after a week in hospital. She had recovered once, then got sick again. Maybe this recovery was another one like the last – a false start, a bad joke, fake news. He passed her a Mars bar.

'Eat something.'

She smiled and took the chocolate. She ate it slowly. Luca knew it was hurting – the plague had left her throat raw and inflamed – but she kept going, forcing down each mouthful until it was all gone.

'The doctors said you need to eat lots,' Luca said. He paused. 'I'm nagging you. Sorry.'

'Don't apologise. It's because you care.'

They drove on in silence, the rain still hammering down so loud, it made conversation difficult. The roads were almost empty, just the odd car passing by. They hadn't seen any Army vehicles since they left the hospital, and there had been only one there parked up outside the emergency department because the mobs were gone. There was nothing left to protest about. It was amazing how quickly the vaccine had been made. Everybody said it was like a miracle, and the scientists who had cracked it deserved a medal. Just luck, the lead scientist had said in his one interview, and Luca could still see Doctor McKenna's eyes as he trotted out that lie, because to even hint at the truth would probably have got him locked up with no chance of ever finding the key.

People were getting better, the vaccine was being delivered to thousands every day, some shops were re-opening. Even the power cuts didn't seem to be too much of a problem. People shrugged and smiled at each other. So what if the lights went out? At least they were still alive. The whole crazy thing seemed like the worst ever nightmare, best forgotten. And as for the bizarre storm that had whipped across London...well, nobody had any explanation for that. A once-in-a-lifetime weather event, they had said on the news. Strong enough to carry huge flocks of birds over the city. And how odd that all those ravens had landed on the Tower...

Yeah, Luca thought. If only you knew.

He touched the swords around his neck – his own and the one that had belonged to Randall. Both were cold, as they had been since that day at the Tower. The day that they had stopped Madoc. The day that something strange happened to Freddie.

They slowed down for a red light. It still freaked him every time he thought about it, which was about once every five minutes when it was dark and quiet and his brain decided to play tricks on him. Just how could a medieval prince who had been dead for more than six hundred years suddenly come alive? Luca shivered and huddled down in his jacket.

Don't overthink it, he told himself, not for the first time. It's over. Move on. Get home.

'You're a better driver than Carter,' he said, remembering the swerving, speeding journey from Winchester to the hospital when his mum had started to get sick again.

'Well, I should hope so.'

'Don't tell him off for nicking the car.'

'He saved my life, Luca. I'm not going to tell him off.'

'Thanks.'

'As long as he puts it back where he found it.'

'If the owner's even alive.'

'He puts it back. And we leave some money for the petrol.'

That was so typical of his mum. After everything she had been through she was still worried what the neighbours might say.

'I bet you've missed them,' she said.

'Yeah. I mean, it's only been a week since I saw them, but they're...well, they're like family now. And you know, I just feel better when I'm with them.'

'I understand. They will have missed you too. Especially Jess.'

His cheeks flushed hot and his mouth dried up.

'Thanks for letting them all stay,' he said, to fill the awkward silence. 'I didn't think Carter would listen when you said trying to get back to Camelot wasn't a good idea.'

'He's a good kid. He knew deep down it was better to stay together. And so did Gwen. You've changed her life, you know that? She now knows what it is to have friends.'

They drove on, quiet again. His mind was on Jess. In that moment when Madoc stabbed him, and the evil magic of that sword was coursing through him like snake venom, she had saved him and told him she loved him. And he loved her so much it almost hurt because he couldn't imagine not being with her, except he knew she would have to leave. She and Freddie couldn't stay forever. Their aunt and uncle were looking after baby Josh now that he was out of hospital. It was only natural that they would go to live there soon.

'Do you think their brother will be okay?' Luca asked.

'Josh?'

'Yeah.'

'Of course. They seemed very sensible people when I phoned. Jess and Freddie need to be with their own family. And it's only an hour away.'

She'll forget all about me, he thought.

He went back to staring out of the window at the rain. There was a tension in the air that he couldn't quite work out – something niggling at him, as if he needed to be ready.

'Go and get some bits for tea,' his mum said, pulling up outside a convenience store. The lights glowed invitingly. 'They'll all be hungry, I expect.'

Without the windscreen wipers on, the glass was immediately a kaleidoscopic blur. Luca was grateful for the chance to get out of the car before his mum said anything else. He didn't want to talk about it any more. Maybe if he ignored it, the problem would go away and the adults would forget it had ever been a plan. He squeezed his mum's arm. It was his lucky routine, something he had done every day in the hospital, just his way of letting her know he was there even when she was too ill to really know much of anything. She smiled and returned the squeeze.

'Jess is lovely, Luca. I like her a lot. Don't worry. Things will work out. They usually do.'

Luca nodded but he didn't say anything. There were some things you just couldn't talk to a parent about. He pulled up his hood and splashed his way to the shop door. It only took a couple of minutes to get the few basics they needed – some bread, long life milk, baked beans and Red Leicester cheese, his mum's favourite. He paused by the chocolate bars and thought of Freddie, and how angry the kid had been when they had left, as if he couldn't deal with it. Was it because of him and Jess, or was there something else going on in his head since that thing with the Black Prince? Luca didn't know and nobody else seemed that bothered about it.

Maybe Jess knows more than she's letting on. Maybe she can still see things.

And then he regretted even thinking something like that. Jess wouldn't hide anything from him. Ever since that bang on the head, no visions of the future. Not even a hint. On the one hand, he was glad because he knew how scary it was for her, but it felt like they had lost something, a way of knowing what might be coming their way and they all felt uneasy about that. Except Freddie, of course. Nothing seemed to bother him.

No, if Jess knew anything, so would he.

He grabbed a few more chocolate bars because mum needed fattening up. She was trying to hide the tiny grimaces of pain when she moved. He would keep giving her the chocolate until that pain was gone.

His phone pinged. He retrieved the stubby black Nokia from his jacket pocket. He was still getting used to buttons instead of a touchscreen but the Ravenmaster had been right when he had ordered the Warders to donate their phones to the children. The battery lasted weeks and you could always get a signal.

He read Jess's text.

Hi

He punched the same back. Nothing specific, just in case. No need to give away anything about them that easily. Who knew whether somebody might be tracking calls and texts?

Hope you ok. You nearly here?

Yes

Have you seen the news?

No. What is it?

She replied immediately.

Bad. Get here asap. X

He paid without a word and raced back to the car, the food stuffed inside his jacket. He held up the screen for his mum to see.

'What do you think?'

'I don't know. Everything has been bad recently. How much worse can it get?'

It took them ten minutes to get to the flat. Carter opened the door as they arrived. His face was grim.

'Madoc's back.'

3

'Welcome home, Mrs B,' Carter said. 'Has he looked after you?'

'Of course,' Liz Broom said. 'More importantly, have you been looking after each other?'

'You bet. I am now officially a domestic warrior. The kettle's on.' Then Carter was hurrying them through the flat. 'Freddie was watching the news. You know, the way he does all day.'

Luca ignored the small talk. His heart was racing and his palms were sweaty. How could Madoc be anywhere but buried at the bottom of the Thames?

'The Prime Minister came on,' Carter continued. 'A press conference about how well it's all going. Then something else.'

The flat was warm, and even though Luca's mind was running at a thousand miles an hour, it felt good to be home again. He glanced into the tiny kitchen. It was clean and tidy. He didn't think that would be down to Carter. He could hear voices from the living room and he suddenly needed more than anything else to see Jess. Then his mum coughed and stumbled beside him. She grabbed for the wall.

'Mum?'

'I'm okay. Just tired.'

'Maybe you should go to bed for a bit.'

'No. I'm fine, honestly.'

'Watch the news later.'

'No. I want to see what's happened.'

Freddie was cross-legged on the floor of the living room. Gwen sat at the small round table in the corner. She looked scared. Jess stood up and hugged Liz, then went to do the same to Luca. He froze, unsure, then he gave her a quick squeeze before settling his mum down in a chair with help from Carter.

'You need to work on that, Romeo,' he whispered.

'Shut up, you idiot,' Luca replied, face burning.

'Just saying. Anyway, welcome back, mate. We've missed you. All of us have.'

'Thanks. Same here.'

'Hello Mrs Broom,' said Freddie. 'You still look unwell. Didn't they at least wait until you were better before they let you out?'

'Try saying something positive for once,' glowered Luca, then immediately regretted it when he saw that Jess was frowning.

Me and my big mouth, he thought.

'It's fine,' Liz said, smiling. 'Freddie's right. Nothing a few more bars of chocolate won't put right, eh?'

She coughed a few times, then it passed.

'Sorry, Freddie,' Luca said.

'I can't help it,' Freddie murmured. 'It's just the way my brain works. And I can't help seeing inside your heads. And I couldn't help it when the Black Prince spoke. I know you all think I could but I couldn't.'

Freddie's voice trailed away, and it was obvious he was close to tears. That shocked Luca. The boy was normally so calm. Something had clearly spooked him.

'Luca didn't mean anything,' Jess said to her brother. 'It's been a long day, yeah? He's tired.'

'He should have just said that. Then I would know.'

'Look, I'm sorry,' Luca repeated. 'I really am. And that thing you just said...about the Black Prince...'

'Another time,' interrupted Carter. 'This is the big news.'

'So is what I just said,' Luca said, angry and frustrated. They had to talk about what had happened at the Tower. Why couldn't any of them see that?

Freddie clicked the remote and suddenly nobody was listening to Luca. The television screen was paused on a grainy image of the Prime Minister. 'Watch.'

On the screen, the Prime Minister adjusted his tie and dabbed at his sweaty top lip.

'Good morning, ladies and gentleman,' he said, glancing around the room.

Luca leaned in close, still seething at Carter's interruption, but it would have to wait for another time. He studied every line on the man's face. He didn't think he'd ever seen someone look so broken. Was it just the Prime Minister's son who had died? Maybe his daughters were gone as well and nobody was admitting it. The Prime Minister swallowed and breathed. The calm arrogant politician was long gone. This was the face of someone who couldn't believe anything any more.

'I'm sorry it's standing room only for most of you,' he said. 'But thank you for coming, all the same. I'm pleased to see so many familiar faces and I want to start by offering my condolences to the families of your colleagues who have died.'

The room was silent. He looked down at the sheets of paper in front of him. He swallowed again, then paused as if to compose himself. Then he began to read.

'As I have said on previous occasions over the past few weeks, this has been the most traumatic event that our great nation has faced since the second world war. There have been dark days and there will be many more ahead, but I can announce today that no new cases of the plague have been reported in the last seventy two hours. This is highly significant, based on what we know of the virus. There is every reason to be cautiously optimistic that we have turned a corner. The vaccine production is going well and we are continuing to deliver thousands of doses across the whole country. If there are no new cases reported over the next three days, we will be very close to winning the battle.'

The silence was shattered by a hundred voices, all firing off questions. The Prime Minister shielded his eyes from the camera flashes.

'What am I waiting for?' asked Luca impatiently.

'Shut up and keep watching,' Carter answered.

On the screen, the Prime Minister was pointing into the audience.

'One at a time, please. John, your question?'

A senior BBC journalist took the offered microphone, unable to hide his pleasure at being singled out for special attention.

'Thank you, sir. And I know how difficult this is for you, with your own family so affected. But how confident are you really that this is getting under control? It certainly doesn't feel like it out there on the streets of our towns and cities.'

'I'm grateful for your kind words. And clearly the loss of so many of our brave police officers, soldiers, civil servants and local authority employees has taken its toll on the civil infrastructure. We are in constant touch with remaining council leaders. Many people are volunteering to help once they have been vaccinated. It will get better, but it will take time. Shops are opening. People are returning to work. I really do believe we are getting there. And of course, no cases have been reported anywhere else in the world so the rapid closure of ports and airports has averted an international catastrophe.'

The questions came thick and fast, a babble of raised voices. The Prime Minister did his best to answer them. It went on and on, then he pointed towards the back of the room.

'Next, please. There, that gentleman at the back. I can't quite see you, sir.'

A shadowy figure stepped forward as the camera cut to him. Freddie pressed the pause button. The figure remained frozen on the screen like a black ghost.

'This is where it gets really interesting.'

'Let it run,' Luca said. His heart was hammering against his chest. He was almost paralysed, unable to move. 'Is that...'

Freddie clicked on play. Before Luca could finish the question, the man moved into full view and stared directly into the nearest camera. His face filled the screen. His eyes burned. His mouth was a tight thin wire and Luca felt a terrible cold chill gripping at his heart.

'Thank you, Prime Minister,' John Madoc said. 'I would like to also add my condolences. I gather all three of your children have now fallen victim to the plague. A terrible tragedy for your family to bear. I'm sure the whole nation shares my admiration for the strength you're showing today, but I have to ask what your government is doing to locate the many people who have gone missing in the chaos, my own daughter being one of them. They, and we, are victims too.'

It took a few seconds for the journalists to register who he was, then pandemonium broke out. Madoc was surrounded. Microphones were thrust at him. The Prime Minister was ashen. His mouth hung open.

'This is a surprise,' he croaked, suddenly. 'We thought...it was assumed...'

'That I was dead? No, sir. I'm very much alive, thank you. A few bruises and a broken leg, that's all. I was very lucky. Many of my employees did not escape that awful fire in the Shard. And that, Prime Minister, is why I'm here today. Will you help me find my daughter, and will you help find the terrorists who took her?'

Freddie hit pause again.

'This can't be happening,' Luca said, his tongue almost glued to the roof of his mouth. He felt sick. 'He fell into the Thames. He stabbed me and then I let go of him. I saw it happen!'

'So?' replied Freddie. 'He survived it.'

'Nobody could have survived that fall.'

Luca rubbed at his hand where Madoc's blade had penetrated, as if the pain of the wound had returned.

'Nobody except him,' said Gwen in a quiet voice.

'Keep going, Freddie,' she said. 'Luca needs to see it all.'

'And so do I,' added Liz.

As the recording continued, Madoc was the centre of attention, commanding the flow of questions. The Prime Minister bluffed his way through, offering his own support to Madoc, and that of course the government would do all it could to help, but he seemed confused and beaten, as if he was no longer in control. The camera panned back to Madoc.

'Thank you, sir. The CCTV at the Shard captured the faces of the youths who took my daughter. I can provide the images for circulation. I'm sure many other buildings will have recorded abductions and worse. We should begin by targeting all those who have taken advantage of the plague to commit foul crimes. The focus should be on the criminals and terrorists. It's the duty of the public to report anybody they suspect of such crimes. We can all help fill the gaps left by our brave dead police.'

Freddie paused the image of Madoc wiping his eyes, but Luca didn't believe there was even the hint of a tear. He wanted to reach into the television and grab him. He wanted to hurt him. He felt the familiar prickle along his back and the red blurring of his vision. His fingers tingled. He was changing.

'More lies!' growled Luca in a voice that was suddenly not all his own. 'He ordered Gwen to be killed with the rest of us!'

His eyes saw different colours, he smelled a thousand odours from beyond a human's range. The lion was taking over again.

'No, Luca. Not this.'

Jess's touch was cool against Luca's cheek. He flinched, then relaxed. Just as quickly as it had threatened to overwhelm him, the animal transformation was gone. He shook his head to get rid of the last traces of it. Where had it come from? Was it going to happen every time he lost his temper? And what would he do if the lion took him over completely...could he be stuck like it forever?

'I can't stop it, Jess. It just happens when I get angry. It's horrible, like I really am an animal.'

'I know. It doesn't matter. You'll find a way to control it. I know you will.'

Luca could see the others were shocked and his mum looked completely horrified, but she thankfully said nothing.

'Mum?'

She bit her lip. Her eyes were wet.

'The first time Peake came, when you were a baby, he said this might happen. I didn't believe him. I didn't want to believe him. Oh, Luca, you looked...you looked like you could kill somebody. Please promise me you never will.'

That was a promise he couldn't make and they all knew it. Liz began to cry and it crushed Luca to see her like that.

'Madoc's very clever, isn't he?' said Freddie, utterly untroubled by what had just occurred.

Luca stared at Freddie. The boy didn't even blink.

'Clever?' Luca said. 'What's clever about it?'

'Think,' Freddie replied, as if he was talking to a child. 'He stands up there and says Gwen's been kidnapped. He asks the whole country to look for the kidnappers. They're all part of his team now. They all want the same thing. Everybody needs an enemy, Luca. He's going to post our faces all over every news site and social media platform. Suddenly, we'll be top of the most wanted list. And when they catch us you can bet Madoc will be there ready to say hello.'

'Freddie's right,' Liz said. 'It's not safe for you here.'

'Give it ten minutes and we'll be trending on Twitter,' added Freddie.

'Then we've got to go,' said Carter. 'All of us.'

'No way,' Luca replied. 'Mum can't go anywhere. She's not well enough. And where would we go anyway?'

'Does it matter?' asked Carter. 'Somewhere nice and quiet. We nick a van, a big car or something. We head on out into the countryside and find an empty house. There's bound to be a few of those around now.'

'You have got to be kidding.'

'Never been more serious.'

Carter stood up. He pointed at the frozen image of Madoc on the screen.

'He's not going to let Gwen go, Luca. He's got some unfinished business with you as well. Oh, and by the way, he's not massive fans of the rest of us. Every minute we sit here talking brings him nearer.'

'And your plan helps, how?'

'We get away from here. He can easily find out where you live. He's bound to come looking.'

'This is crazy.'

'Like every day of my life since I met you.'

'Might be a good time to fly again,' said Freddie, pulling out a squashed chocolate bar. 'Can't you call Bran and his friends?'

And the room was silent except for the sound of his chewing.

4

'That went well, sir,' murmured Gabriel as he followed his boss out of the press conference. The clamour of noise was showing no sign of settling. Now that the Prime Minister was back in charge of the microphone, the questions were coming faster than ever.

'Thank you,' Madoc said. 'I think the Prime Minister was suitably surprised to see me. And I'm sure he'll be kept busy in there for a while.

'Why didn't he have you arrested, sir? You know, with all three of his kids dead.'

'Good question,' Madoc chuckled.

'You must have something on him. No other reason.'

'Best not to know, Gabriel. Leave my dirty secrets to me, eh?'

'Yes, sir.'

Now, does the next idiot know where to meet us?'

'Yes.'

'Good. Straight there, then.'

A few journalists had followed, keen to get an extra exclusive, but Gabriel opened his jacket to reveal a pistol.

'You can't just walk around armed, mate,' one of them shouted.

'Try and stop me,' Gabriel replied as he guided Madoc into a black car with no number plates. They were away in seconds.

'Was that wise?' Madoc asked.

'It shows them not to come looking. Everything's changed, sir. The plague has seen to that. The only rule left is that there aren't any rules.'

'I hope you're right.'

They drove on in silence. Gabriel doubled back a few times then he cut down a dozen side-alleys and one way streets, all the time heading east out of the city. He finally parked up between two equally anonymous cars. He got out, checked all was clear then tapped on the window. Madoc scrambled awkwardly onto the tarmac.

'Damn leg,' he muttered, testing his weight. The pain was worse than it had been for days. The climb up the Shard hadn't helped, but there had been no choice. Now that he had the spell book again, it was time to move to the next stage of his plan.

A steady cold drizzle began to fall, soaking his hair and face. In no time, the pavements were glistening wet. Most of the street lights were smashed and those that were intact didn't work. The power wasn't on in this part of London, far from the wealthy west. Madoc followed Gabriel into the disused industrial unit that had been their base for the last month. Once they were inside and the steel shutters were bolted, Gabriel fired up the generator and flicked on the heaters. A comforting yellow light filled the whole space. Madoc slumped into a chair, facing the door but far enough back to be in shadow. He glanced at the second, less obvious door off to his right. Gabriel had done a good job. This place was secure, it was warm, they were fed thanks to his seemingly endless ability to find enough to eat, and he had even rigged up screens to provide Madoc with a bedroom, of sorts. The bathroom arrangements weren't exactly what he was used to but the unit had served a purpose. It had been important to stay off the radar until he was ready to act. And now that he was, this place would soon be nothing but a brief memory. Before that happened, there was one more person he needed to meet.

He glanced at the yellow hospital waste bags in the corner. He had never asked Gabriel where he had found all the bandages and medicines. He didn't care. All that mattered was that because of them, Madoc's leg was healing in a decent position, he had taken antibiotics for any infection and he had been able to control the pain from his wounds.

Madoc stood up and stretched, restless and impatient. Gabriel had found a safe from somewhere and cemented it to the floor at the far end of the unit. Madoc stroked the cold metal and spun the wheel back and forth until the door clicked open. He didn't remove the spell book. He just needed to see it. Satisfied, he closed and locked the door. Then he went back to the chair. He was more tired than he had realised, and soon he was drifting in and out of sleep.

Madoc woke with a start. He had slept for an hour. His mouth tasted horrible, like wet cardboard. Gabriel had put a bottle of water and some paracetamol next to him and Madoc slurped down the painkillers. Gabriel was over by the shutter, gun in hand, whispering through a small hatch. He pulled back the bolt and then, in an instant, sprang back into a firing position. A man entered the unit and his hands were high above his head.

'Good evening, Mr Johnson,' Madoc said to the most senior policeman in the United Kingdom, the Commissioner of the Metropolitan Police. 'Please take a seat.'

Madoc gestured to a small uncomfortable looking chair directly opposite him.

'I would offer you some refreshments but as you can, my situation is rather diminished.'

Johnson moved slowly, eyes darting around the place, hands still up. Gabriel walked casually behind. Johnson sat down.

'No games, Madoc,' he said. 'Just tell me what this is all about. I don't want to be here a minute longer than I have to.'

'Now, is that any way to greet an old friend?'

'I've never called you a friend. In fact, there's no record that you and I have ever met.'

'Maybe not in your official police files, Johnson,' Madoc smiled, 'but your secret bank account tells a different story.'

Johnson swallowed hard. He was a big man, but he seemed to shrink in that room. His shoulders sagged down. He blinked nervously. He played with his hands, fingers locking and unlocking.

'Let's not pretend that this is anything other than payback time,' said Madoc.

'I...I...' the man stammered, eyes even wider, 'I don't know what you mean.'

'Don't play games. At least the criminals don't pretend to be anything else.'

The Commissioner's mouth worked up and down but no words came out. He started to stand up but Madoc shook his head and looked at Gabriel who was leaning passively against the wall, inspecting his fingernails.

'Your thug doesn't scare me,' Johnson said, sinking back into the chair.

'Really?' Madoc replied. 'He should. Now, to business. I'm bored of you already. I want you to find my daughter.'

'You said she'd been kidnapped when you photo bombed the PM's press conference. I'm surprised he let you go after that performance. Is he another one with dirty money in his pockets?'

'How could you imagine such a thing?'

Johnson looked away in disgust.

'You're all the same when the fifty pound notes flutter down from the sky,' Madoc whispered. 'And she has been kidnapped, in a way. These children managed to convince her that she belongs with them and not her father. I need to convince her otherwise.'

'Madoc, there are barely enough officers left to protect the government and Royal Family. I can't just order a large number of them to go looking for your daughter.'

'She's not as important as the brain dead politicians who pretend they're in charge? And as for that bunch of frauds in Windsor castle...'

'It would be impossible to order it without raising suspicions.'

'You'll find a way. I can give you names and descriptions. Start off by looking in Winchester. They might be there. I want them all caught. Understand?'

Johnson nodded miserably.

'And there's one more job I need you to do. The reward for all of this will be my eternal gratitude and another million pounds in your slush fund.'

Now Johnson sat up, greed overtaking fear.

'I can see we're suddenly talking the same language,' Madoc continued. 'There's someone else you need to find.

'Who?'

'An old woman by the name of Angela Morgan.'

'I've never heard of her.'

'Of course you haven't, you imbecile. She's not famous. However, she is important beyond belief. Find her and that's your million pounds.'

The unit was silent except for the hum of the generator and Gabriel whistling softly.

'That's all I get? A name?'

'Yes. And you can of course leave whenever you want. Nobody's stopping you.'

Johnson breathed deeply. His face was pale. He blinked rapidly.

'I'll find all of them. You have my word.'

'That's very kind of you,' Madoc said. He stood up, ignoring the pain in his leg. He leaned towards the man, enjoying the fear.

'You have seventy two hours. And I can easily arrange for your wife and children to disappear if you don't.'

A silence, a horrible pause as Madoc's words sank in, then Johnson scrambled out of there as if he was escaping from a sinking ship.

'Pathetic,' Madoc said, staring at the steel door. 'Supposed to be in charge of London. I wouldn't trust him with my socks.'

'You're right,' replied Gabriel, 'but he'll do the business. No way he won't. Did you see his eyes? Like a frightened rabbit.'

'A rabbit that I need, Gabriel. I can threaten more than I can act at the moment. Just because I know all his deepest darkest secrets doesn't mean he might not decide to call my bluff. Now, I want to get out of here. I want a shower and a proper bed for the night. Are we set?'

'Yes, sir. Nice house, quiet and out of the way. And there'll be no trace of you here.'

Madoc retrieved the spell book from the safe and left without a backward glance. The unit was already burning fiercely as they drove away. He cradled his treasure, holding it firmly, focused on what he would have to do. And he knew, deep down, he was excited and terrified in equal measure.

5

The shadows hid the two men from any casual glances. Shorty, the one with the brains and the delicate fingers that could open any lock ever invented, sniffed the damp air and nudged his taller colleague in the ribs.

'Footsteps. He's here.'

The taller man, whose name was Tallboy for exactly that reason, didn't have the brains but did have fists like big hams which he enjoyed using when he was told to, nodded and grinned for no reason other than he couldn't think of anything to say. Words rarely appeared on his lips. All his talking happened just beyond his wrists, and the language was usually quick, loud and violent.

Tallboy kept grinning and nodding, nodding and grinning. The wheel's turning but the hamster's dead, Shorty had said to him once, and Tallboy had laughed because it sounded funny, not because he understood that Shorty was describing the empty space inside his skull. It didn't matter. He wasn't there to win a pub quiz. He was there to intimidate.

'And lose the stupid grin,' Shorty added.

The grin disappeared as if his mate had thrown a switch, and Tallboy's face was suddenly much scarier. The long pale scar from forehead to chin dragged the corner of his mouth into a twisted curl. One broken

35

tooth peeked out between chewed lips. His eyes, like a pig's, were black and beady. He stood completely still, waiting to be told what to do next.

Shorty sniffed the air again just as a man turned into the alleyway. His silhouette was hunched and nervous, a blurred mixture of jumpy steps and rapid backward glances. Shorty smiled. That was a good sign. The man clearly didn't want to be there. He would agree to anything just to get away from this part of town.

'Over here,' Shorty whispered.

The man stopped, hesitant, ready to run.

'I can't see you,' he said.

'I know. Just keep walking, Commissioner. You're in the right place. Down the end, where it's dark.'

The man didn't move.

'Come on,' Shorty hissed. 'We haven't got all night. There might be scary people around.'

That seemed to help. The man shuffled along, head still down and shoulders hunched over, trying to be invisible and looking for all the world like somebody with something to hide. He stood about two metres from Shorty, his face tight against the cold. Shorty waited. He wasn't really in a hurry. It was better to let the client speak first. They usually panicked and showed their best hand. This one was no different.

'Are we alone?'

Shorty motioned with his hands.

'No, I've hidden all my Instagram followers behind that wheelie bin.'

Commissioner Johnson looked bemused. Shorty sighed and rolled his eyes.

'Of course we're alone, you idiot. Bloody hell, how did you ever get to be in charge of the Met? You're as dumb as him.'

He flicked his thumb at Tallboy, who started nodding and grinning again. Johnson sucked on his teeth, clearly unused to being insulted but unable to do much about it.

'Enough of the wisecracks,' he whispered. 'I want you to find someone.'

'What's the magic word?' Shorty asked.

'Abracadabra?'

'Try again. And it's not please.'

'I'm guessing it's money.'

'Top of the class. You get a shiny sticker. Now who are we looking for and how much is it worth?'

'Five thousand now. For expenses. Another fifteen thousand when you find her.'

'Keep talking.'

'Her name's Angela Morgan. She'll be about seventy five. Maybe older. Lived all over. Disappeared off the grid about forty years ago. I've searched but nothing shows up at all on phone records, social media, you name it. Like she never existed.'

Shorty paused and scratched his head.

'Interesting. A lady who doesn't want to be found. And the smart minds at Scotland Yard have drawn a blank.'

Johnson smiled nervously.

'But you gentleman have other ways. You know people. You can rummage in the haystack and find the needle.'

'Yep. And for that, it'll cost you more than a piddling fifteen grand.'

'How much?'

'Fifty.'

'What? Are you insane?'

'Come on,' Shorty hissed. 'The world's changed, or haven't you noticed? You wouldn't come down here unless you wanted her found very badly. Fifty thousand in cash, take it or leave it.'

'I...I don't have the authority to make that kind of decision.'

Shorty threw his head back and laughed like a hyena, not caring who might hear.

'You don't? Then who's pulling your puppet strings?'

Johnson looked away, agitated.

'Keep the noise down, will you?'

'No,' said Shorty, suddenly very serious. He leaned in close, eyes narrowed, gold teeth glinting like tiny suns. 'Fifty thousand, big shot Commissioner. Yes or no.'

Silence for a few moments. Nothing between them but the distant sounds of a city trying to get back to normal.

'Well?'

'You're enjoying this, aren't you?'

'Yep, I am. The first time we met you were a detective sergeant with his fingers in lots of dodgy pies who was happy to take a few quid to look the other way. Now you're the super cop, the *numero uno*, the knight of the realm, but down here we're exactly the same. Just trying to survive. So meet my price and we'll find her for you. If you don't, we'll walk away. Simple as that.'

Tallboy cracked his knuckles.

'You tell him, Shorty. Tell him you're in charge now.'

'Shut up,' Shorty snarled, not taking his eyes off the man in front of him. 'So, like I said, meet my price.'

Johnson nodded and back away. He half turned when he was nearly out of the alley.

'I could get another couple of nobodies to do it for twenty thousand.'

'You could try. Any half decent criminal not dead from the plague has long since left town.'

'So why are you and no brains still here?'

'Fair question,' chuckled Shorty. 'Maybe I just had a feeling that my luck was about to change. And here you are, rolling me two sixes. We'll be in touch.'

And with that, their conversation was at an end. As the Commissioner disappeared from view, a massive black bird swooped across Shorty's head. He ducked, unsure, but the bird was gone, almost as if it had never been there at all.

6

There were just four windows in the windmill, one for each full turn of the stairs, and each one no bigger than a face, so that hardly any light found its way into the ancient building even when the glass was clean, which hadn't been the case for a long time. The cobwebs over the windows were so thick they could have been tacked up blankets.

There was one door at the base of the mill. The frame was warped by sea and sun, and the door either stuck or swung open seemingly at random. There was a certain knack to shoving and lifting it at the same time. Otherwise, the door just sat there like a stubborn donkey. Over the years, countless feet had worn a groove under the door, so there was plenty of room for the rats who lived among the shadows. They came and went as they pleased. So did the wind and the rain. Nevertheless, the windmill survived because it had been built to do just that.

A thirteen year old girl by the name of Freya lived there, and she didn't mind the door or the rats. In fact, she liked to hear them scuttling about. The sounds comforted her through the long dark nights, miles from anything or anyone.

She smudged her hand across the kitchen window but all that did was move some of the dirt and cobwebs from one side to the other. She tried again. A thick smear of grime sat stubbornly at one corner but at least she could now see the cold, sour unwelcoming landscape of black and grey sea and sky. The skinny horses who wandered around in the mud were grey, and so were Freya's eyes. The colour of moonlight, her nan had called them, before the whispers began and she had to leave them. Freya missed her nan. Without her, the world was a lonelier place.

'Need to clean them on the outside,' Freya said, smacking her fist against the frame. Not the glass, mind. She wasn't stupid. A sharp blow would probably break the pane, and she was in no mood to walk the five miles into town to steal a replacement. Instead, she hit the wood, which was nearly as fragile as the glass. It squeaked and crunched. Freya paused. She held her hand out, feeling for a fresh draught. It seemed okay, so she punched the dirty limestone wall instead.

'Ouch.'

That had hurt, and fresh blood oozed from her scabbed knuckles. Maybe the pain would help her to stay awake because these days, sleep was always bad. That was when he visited her dreams, looking for her. He wanted to be king, this man with his dark eyes and terrible anger.

Four weeks ago she had stood in a strange dazed stupor and smelled a burning building, and heard the screams and shouts of ravens and children. She didn't know what it was she was seeing, or whether it was real or imagined, but she did know that these children had beaten the dark eyed man with shining swords and something more powerful than hate. She sensed the love they had for each other and she envied them such a thing.

And for four weeks she had dreamed of the man and every morning she woke with tears drying on her cheeks because he was getting closer.

The radio crackled and hissed. The signal was poor on a good day, so now, with the wind roaring in from the east and the rain hitting the windmill like a hundred million razor blades, there was nothing but static. That didn't matter. Freya had heard enough before the weather closed in. She knew what it meant. The man was called Madoc. He had asked the public to find his daughter and the children who had taken her, but Freya knew that was a lie. Adults were good at lying. They did it all the time. She sobbed, the sudden sound catching in her throat, surprising her with its intensity.

'No,' she whispered, wiping her bleeding hand across dry eyes. No way was she going to cry. No way.

She lit a candle and sank into the ugly old chair that had been her mum's favourite. Her hand slipped down the side of the greasy cushion. Her fingers closed around cold steel and she breathed out, counting to ten silently in her mind, regulating her breathing and slowing her heart rate. Shooting wildly was useless. She would have to stay calm. And who would come first, the men sent by Madoc to find her or the ones who had no idea of what they were mixed up in? She wasn't sure she cared too much either way. Ambrose had told her it was time for her to be a part of it all. She knew he was right, but that didn't mean she had to like it. Whoever invaded her world might have to pay a high price for doing so.

A few hours later, when darkness closed over the marsh, the pain in her knuckles dulled down to nothing, Freya's eyes drooped, and even though she fought to stay awake there was nothing she could do.

7

After a long and loud argument, it was agreed that if they were going to leave Winchester, the best direction was west. At least they would be heading away from London and towards Lundy. They had to get the swords working again and nobody had any idea how except to take them back to Camelot.

'So, how are we going to get there?' Gwen asked. 'It's not exactly on a direct bus route.'

'The ravens could take us.'

Gwen shook her head, not wanting to encourage Freddie. She liked him, of course, but sometimes he was just a bit too weird. They weren't going to fly to Camelot. In fact, she had serious doubts as to whether they should be going there at all. Now that she knew her father (and it hurt to even think of him as that) was alive, all Gwen wanted to do was run away, but Camelot was too obvious a place to hide. He would send his people to find them. He would hunt them down.

And yet...

Gwen touched the cold sword nestling against her skin. Nothing from any of the swords since they had stood over the final raven in the tower. All of them cold and dead and useless. They had to get them working again but Camelot hadn't been pleased to see her the first time so why should it be any different now?

'The swords,' Freddie whispered, tapping into her thoughts.

'We can't fly,' she said. 'We just can't.'

'Gwen's right,' added Luca, rescuing her from any more of Freddie's probing. 'How do we even call the ravens?'

'You and Bran are supposed to be friends.'

Sulky Freddie this time, voice low and bottom lip out. Gwen noticed that Jess gave Luca a look that meant please go easy on him, he means well, he just doesn't always understand how other people think and feel. She envied Jess and Luca. They clearly adored each other but were struggling to find a way to be relaxed about it. It was lovely and frustrating at the same time. She wondered, for probably the thousandth time, if she would ever feel such love for anybody. Her mum was gone. Her father...

No, she thought. John Madoc is not my father. My father is dead to me.

She glanced at Carter. He grinned his usual big goofy grin. She had to look away. There were bigger questions to be answered and she understood what was ahead. Difficult times. Maybe terrible times.

I don't want to get hurt again. And if I lose Carter, or any of these incredible people, the hurt will be too much to bear.

And thinking that was painful enough.

'Bran and me, well, we *are* friends, Freddie,' Luca continued, and he seemed to be trying hard to soften his tone. 'I can't exactly text him, though.'

Luca tried a smile but Freddie didn't seem to get the joke. Instead, he held up his sword.

'It's because these are broken, I think. Like if you crack the screen on your iPhone.'

'Yeah,' Luca sighed. 'Something like that. It's all the swords' fault.'

Nice try, thought Gwen, feeling for Luca. It must be tough being appointed some kind of leader, future king, whatever the hell you want to call it, and now he's got to deal with that monster still being alive. How could we have ever imagined it was over?

'I just thought, you know, with you being the Pendragon, that you would know what to do.'

'That's enough, Freddie,' said Jess, mouthing a silent sorry at Luca.

Gwen watched for his reaction. Not anger, which would have been the natural thing. No, he was calm and thoughtful, and most wonderfully, he was caring more about Jess than he was about himself.

'I can steal a van,' Carter suggested, direct as always. 'Really, it's no big deal.'

Gwen couldn't help but laugh out loud. Trust Carter to chuck in something like that.

'No more stealing, thank you,' Liz said.

'Borrow, then.'

'No.'

'Carter's right, mum,' said Luca. 'We need wheels.'

Carter was pointing through the window at a battered Land Rover about fifty metres away.

'That'll do.'

'No,' Liz said. 'The owner's called Ken. He walks his dog past here twice a day. He always says hello. He's a nice man. We can't steal his car.'

'I haven't seen anybody walking a dog all the time we've been here. Which is his flat?'

'He might be dead in there,' said Jess.

'Yeah. And so the Land Rover keys will be in there with him.'

'Is this what we've come to?' muttered Liz.

'You said yourself we can't stop here. Just being practical.'

And there was nothing else to say. They grabbed their coats and headed for the door. Liz protested again but Luca just shook his head.

'No choice, mum. Let's go.'

'Have you got the photo? We might never come back here.'

'In my pocket. Always.'

Gwen knew what that photo meant to Luca. It was the only one he had of him with his dad. She imagined one of herself and the man who had betrayed her in the most terrible way, and all she could think about was burning it in front of his face.

Outside the flat, the wind sliced across them and the air was damp with cruel drizzle. Winchester suddenly didn't feel far enough away from London to be safe. A woman hurried past them. She was carrying a baby. She stared at them, then carried on, then glanced back when she was a fair distance away.

Carter grabbed Gwen's arm.

'I'm going in to get the keys. You with me?'

'Absolutely.'

Ken's flat door was locked but it was no match for some well-aimed kicks. Carter barreled in first and Gwen followed, holding her breath. The air was cold and stale with a strong whiff of dog biscuits but it wasn't too unpleasant. She relaxed, but only slightly. She was ready to defend herself if necessary.

'Anybody home?' Carter shouted.

No reply, which was either good or bad, depending on what they wanted to find. Carter swerved into the kitchen. Gwen headed into the living room. It was dark in there and she stepped back, not wanting to be attacked from behind. Her heart was beating quickly. She thought of the service station where Carter had been attacked and she tensed, fists ready. Carter was suddenly right behind her and she spun around, ready to punch.

'Easy. Found anything?'

'Just you and your foghorn mouth,' she hissed. 'I nearly hit you.'

'Luckily for me you didn't.'

He pushed past into the room and flicked the light on. There was a sofa, an armchair and a dog bed next to a small table covered in newspaper and pieces of a half-finished model ship. As Gwen's eyes adjusted, she saw a shelf on the far wall with another dozen ships, each one beautifully painted. A photograph of some sailors was propped up at one end of the shelf, a group of smiling young men who Gwen guessed would be Ken and his mates.

A sudden pang of sadness gripped her. Nobody had been in the flat for days, that was obvious, and it was likely Ken was dead or very sick. Where was he now? And what happened to his dog? She thought of the man's family. She thought of what her father had done to so many people and the sadness was replaced by cold fury.

'Got them,' Carter said, holding up a bunch of keys as if they were an Olympic medal.

Gwen mouthed a silent apology to the smiling sailors and followed Carter out of the flat. They helped Liz into the driver's seat, and even though she was really too weak to drive there was no way she was going to let Carter behind the wheel. He started to argue but there was no point. It was part of the deal. Luca scrambled in next to her and the others took the back seats, Gwen and Carter on one side, Freddie and Jess facing them.

'Seat belts on, please,' Liz said.

The ignition chugged and chugged, reluctant to fire up, but Land Rovers are built to last and this one was in good shape. The engine caught.

'I hope we can bring it back one day,' Liz said, looking towards Ken's flat, then they were off.

They passed the woman with the baby, and Gwen's eyes met hers. She was talking into her phone and she looked anxious. Gwen's gut told her they might be in trouble.

'I think she's onto us.'

Freddie leaned forwards, fixing on the woman, concentrating hard.

'Yeah. I can hear how scared she is. She's guessed who we are. She's calling the police.'

'As quickly as that?' Luca asked. 'This is bad. They could be just around the corner.'

'They are,' Freddie replied. 'Listen.'

Nothing except for the rumble of the old diesel engine and their breathing, and they drove on for maybe five minutes, but Freddie kept glancing around, frowning.

'They're coming. They really are.'

Then Gwen heard a siren in the distance, getting closer. More than one, by the sound of it.

'Told you.'

'This is *really* bad,' said Luca.

Gwen couldn't disagree. She was shocked at how quickly the police seemed to be responding, but then she remembered how powerful her father was. Nothing had ever stopped him before so there was no reason for this to be different. The sirens were now in front and behind. The Land Rover slowed down.

'What are you doing?' Carter shouted. 'Faster!'

'Give me a moment,' Liz said. 'I need to think.'

Then she turned into a side street, then turned again and parked up behind a row of garages. She turned off the engine. The sirens were growing louder by the second.

'This isn't going to work,' she said. 'Luca, all of you, go on foot. Head into town, keep hidden. I'll try and lead them away from you.'

'Not a chance,' Luca said. 'We're not leaving you.'

'You have to. I'm not strong enough to keep up.'

Liz continued to argue even as they helped her out of the Land Rover.

'We'll carry you,' Luca continued.

The sirens had stopped, but Gwen could hear voices. The police were close, presumably trying to work out if the phone call was a hoax or a false alarm. Then an officer in a high-viz jacket walked past the bottom of the road and stared straight at them. He immediately grabbed his radio and called it in. Two more officers appeared within ten seconds.

'Got any bright ideas?' Carter asked.

'Of course,' said Freddie. 'Just do nothing. Can't you feel what's coming?'

Gwen looked up. The sky was suddenly much darker and the officers' shouts seemed lost in a new rushing roar. The wind had picked up from nowhere. They were all struggling to stay on their feet. Gwen grabbed Carter's hand, holding on against the buffeting roaring wind. Then she heard a noise she recognised. It was the screams of ravens.

'Look!'

She couldn't tell who had shouted, because her head was full of too much noise, but she looked up again just the same. A huge black cloud was surging towards them. It swallowed up the officers. Their fluorescent jackets were no more than flashes of colour in the maelstrom. Then the cloud was on them. She ducked against the onslaught, her eyes closed, feathers tickling her face, claws pulling her hair. The smell was intense – a meaty ammonia that stung her nostrils. The screams were so loud she had to clamp her hands across her ears.

Then the cloud of ravens lifted up and away, and they were stood in the centre of a swirling funnel of birds. The officers were nowhere to be seen, and Gwen had just enough time to wonder how they would ever explain what had just happened before a man emerged through the ravens as easily as if he had slid through a fine curtain of mist.

He was tall and thin, with white swept back hair and piercing eyes. A huge raven sat on his shoulder.

'Bran!' shouted Luca.

The raven screamed out a greeting. The man smiled.

'Ladies and gentleman, it would appear we need to be elsewhere.'

He clicked his fingers. The funnel of birds closed around them and lifted them up into the air and they were surging through the night sky at a speed that was impossible to believe.

8

Madoc was dozing in a chair in the front room of the comfortable but anonymous London townhouse that Gabriel had found. The people who lived there weren't coming back, Gabriel had assured him and Madoc had not asked how he could be so sure. He didn't need to know. He didn't want to know. They were south of the river, his bed was comfortable, the lights worked and the shower ran hot. There was food in the fridge and a powerful car parked outside in case a quick getaway was needed. Yet again, Gabriel had done everything asked of him and more.

Madoc shifted in his sleep. He didn't dream often and when he did the dreams were usually ones of good things like money and power, but now his dream was an unsettling collage, flitting from image to image. He was surrounded by birds and people. The people were pointing at him. Their eyes were black. They turned and looked up and he did the same. The Shard towered over him, an ugly mess of smoke and flames. Madoc blinked and he was inside the building, looking down from the round table in his office as if he was the painted face of the king. Then the windows were gone and he was on a narrow balcony, high over the city. He fell into the freezing Thames and the water crushed him. He gasped and woke up, heart pounding, breathing ragged.

Gabriel was leaning over him.

'Good news, sir,' he said.

It took Madoc a few moments to clear his thoughts. The dream had been so real. Those people, their eyes...

'News? What news?'

'Police report children matching their descriptions in Winchester. Strange event. Sudden storm, lots of big black birds, a man appearing out of nowhere and then they were all gone, just like.'

'Merlin's back.'

'If you say so.'

'I do. He'll take them to Camelot. I know he will.'

'I don't have the men or the equipment to go back there.'

'You don't need to. They'll have to surface at some point. And if Merlin's around again I can guess where it might be. What about Johnson. Have you heard from him?'

'Just now. He's on the way here.'

'Really? Has he found the woman?'

'He wouldn't tell me.'

'What an idiot.'

Madoc shook his head, washing away the last traces of the dream. He didn't want Gabriel to see how rattled he was. It had just been a dream. He had escaped the river. And those people...well, they were all dead.

An hour later, Gabriel was escorting Commissioner Johnson into the room. They looked like prisoner and jailer, and that immediately cheered Madoc up. The usual order of things was continuing – he was in charge, and the rich and the powerful did as he ordered. He gave the Commissioner his special smile, the one he reserved for those he respected the least.

'So, are you soon to be a million pounds richer? I hope so, because if you've come here to beg for more time, you already know the response you'll get.'

'I've found her,' the Commissioner said, suddenly smiling himself, but the flickering eyelids and tremble in his voice betrayed how scared he was.

'Impressive,' Madoc whispered, and he meant it. Giving this idiot three days to track down a woman who had no intention of being found by anyone had been a big ask. Gabriel had guessed it might take two weeks or more, especially in the chaos of a post plague London.

'Actually, I've found more than her, because the woman you want is dead.'

Johnson paused, growing in confidence. Madoc waited, unblinking. Johnson's smile faded. The confidence was suddenly gone.

'She died twenty years ago,' he croaked. 'In Spain. She moved there, changed her name and lived quietly in a small village in the mountains. But she had a son, and he was easy to find. Military records are always the easiest to hack.'

Madoc leaned forwards in his chair. This was unexpected news.

'Go on.'

'His name was David Morgan. Exemplary record, and when he retired he was recommended as a Yeoman Warder at the Tower of London. He served with distinction until his recent death. Caught in the crossfire of random shootings near the Gherkin. Just before the unexplained storm that brought the ravens to London.'

Now this was something worth listening to, and although Madoc feigned indifference he was already trying to work out what this could mean. The dead soldier must have known about his mother. Were there other insiders he didn't know about? Who else might be helping his daughter?

'He was the one with the children,' Gabriel said. 'I shot him as he came up out of the sewers.'

'I can work that bit out for myself,' Madoc snapped irritably, 'but he's dead and we'll never know any more about him.'

In spite of his obvious fear, Johnson smiled again. A prickle of anger passed down Madoc's spine. He had to fight back an irrational urge to grab the policeman by the lapels and shake him.

'You seem to find this funny.'

'No, Madoc. Not funny. But I do have more to tell you. Your dead soldier had a wife and daughter.'

Now the prickles on Madoc spine rolled up and down like crashing waves, and it wasn't anger he felt but pure excitement. If this was true...

'Where are they?'

'The wife is missing. My sources have done some serious digging. Took a lot of work and a lot of money.'

Madoc ignored the hint. This fool was going to be paid enough to cover a few bribes. Johnson shrugged and carried on.

'Maybe she's dead as well. Lots of people are. Anyway, the daughter is somewhere in Kent. The best lead I've got points towards the marshes, right out in the middle of nowhere. It'll take a bit more time but we'll find her soon.'

'Kent, eh? Where?'

'Dungeness. Bleak place. Not exactly number one on Trip Advisor.'

'Who are your people?'

'Criminals with fingers in lots of pies. What they don't know isn't worth knowing. Experts in fraud, burglary, extortion, internet crime, money laundering and violence. Especially the violence.'

'I like them already. Update me as soon as you know anything new. And I gather my daughter and her friends escaped from Winchester.'

'Yes. A strange affair. The officers swear they saw a column of ravens carry them off into the sky. Impossible, of course. I have no idea what happened.'

'So the police failed.'

'Failed? It's chaos out there, Madoc. Forget what the Prime Minister said. Gangs are running the streets. Nobody goes out after dark. The police are doing the best they can in very difficult circumstances.'

'That sounds like an excuse why you haven't found her, rather than a reason why you can't.'

For the first time, anger flashed across the Commissioner's face.

'Get real. Look around you. It's all very well pretending you rule the world from your squatter's paradise, but it's not that simple. If the PM suspects I'm working with you, I'll quietly disappear in a heartbeat. His children died, remember? You're definitely off his Christmas card list.'

Gabriel raised an eyebrow. Madoc shook his head. It wasn't quite the time to get rid of Johnson. He was still useful.

'I don't want to see or hear from you until you've got this girl. Understand?'

'Clearly.'

Madoc clenched his fists until the nails bit into the skin. Johnson left without another word.

'Gabriel, get a message out to any of my people you can contact down there. See what we can find out. I want regular updates. And I want to leave this house. Find me somewhere in Canterbury.'

'Why Canterbury?'

'You don't need to know, yet.'

'Yes, sir. And what about your daughter?'

Madoc smiled.

'Well, everything is suddenly clearer. I have a feeling we won't need to look for her, or her friends. Something tells me that they will find us.'

9

Luca didn't know where he was or what had happened – there was nothing but a terrifying blankness that might never go away. He scrambled around and he felt warm sand between his fingers. He heard the echoing cries of ravens close by and far away. He looked all around, and realisation dawned. The others were there as well, sprawled on the long beach that led down to the inky black lake. He bumped against the statue of Arthur. They were back at Camelot. Feathers drifted down like black snowflakes.

'What...what...how...?'

His mum was crawling towards him, looking like she might faint.

'Bran,' was all he could say, because that was the last thing he could really recall. 'I saw Bran.'

Then he remembered the woman with the baby, the Land Rover, the police in their high-viz jackets closing in on them, and the man...

'Who was he?'

'Not a clue,' Carter asked, brushing sand and feathers off his jeans.

'It's obvious,' said Freddie. 'Peake, but not Peake any more.'

'Correct, young man.'

They turned and stared at a cave, which Luca wasn't sure had been there a moment ago, but like so much else he couldn't be sure about that either. The tall man emerged, his hands clasped behind his back. Bran hopped along the sand beside him, chattering and clacking, wings outstretched. The raven flopped up to Luca and rubbed his head against his legs. Luca reached down and stroked the bird's head. Suddenly, his headache didn't seem so bad, and the sand wedged in his teeth was easier to ignore.

'Hello, mate,' he said. 'I've really missed you. Any chance you can explain what the hell is going on?'

Bran cackled and his eyes gleamed, and Luca could have sworn the raven was laughing at him. Why not? Everything else was utterly crazy, so a laughing bird fitted in just right.

'Please don't be alarmed,' the man said as he picked his way across the sand towards them. 'I can understand how confusing this is.'

Carter looked ready for a fight. Gwen rested a hand on his arm. Jess and Freddie were silent, watching every move. Luca's mum leaned against him. She coughed and held her chest.

'We're at Camelot, mum,' Luca said. 'It's okay. Just breathe slowly. We're safe here.'

'Is that Peake?' she asked in between coughs. 'And did that journey just happen?'

'Yes, Liz, it's me,' said the man, who was now among them and apparently unconcerned at Carter's posturing, 'and I hope you are recovering your strength. I didn't think you would survive, and I'm very pleased to have been proved wrong.'

Luca stared, trying to make sense of it. The tall man didn't look like Peake, or sound like him, or move like him, but he was here and he knew his mum's name. The man lifted from his coat the ugly gargoyle that Peake had always worn.

'My new name is Ambrose. It's happened many times before and it will happen again. I've been men, and women, boys and girls, black and white and all the races of the earth. I've even been an animal or two down the years.' Ambrose chuckled. 'I once spent a very pleasant century as a blue whale, but that's a story for another day.'

He gestured for them to follow him down to the bridge across the lake. He paused at the spot where he had hurled himself against Madoc's men and then disappeared into the foaming lake.

'Tell me everything that happened after I left. Everything.'

***

'It's worse than I thought,' Ambrose said. 'You've got a lot of work ahead.'

There had been lots of talking and more than a bit of shouting. Ambrose had listened to it all and responded as best as he said he could, and now, after everything that needed to be said was said, the mood was calm. Ambrose turned to Gwen, his face stern.

'Your father will do anything to get the power he craves,' he said, 'and if he tries what I think he might, your next test is going to be even more dangerous than saving the ravens.'

That didn't sound good and they all said so. Ambrose silenced them with a cough.

'I think you all need to listen a bit more and talk a bit less,' said Liz.

'Well said. Sensible advice.'

The light in the cavern had changed from gentle orange to deep cold purple, and even the lake seemed to be restless. Circles spread out across the surface and bubbles rose up from the unknown depths. Luca hadn't really considered there might be things in there. What kind of creature could live in an underground lake next to a magical castle? He decided he didn't want to know.

'Go on, then,' he said, still unsure how he felt about the changed man in front of them. Was he still Peake or was he a completely different person? Or maybe they were just bits of the same, and that's why they were so different, like a toe is different from an ear. It was just something else to process in their new crazy world.

'You will have noticed that your swords are dead,' said Ambrose. 'Cold, unresponsive. Used up. That's because you used all of their power when you tried to save the final raven.'

'So, we just put them on the Round Table again.'

'Oh, Luca, it's not that straightforward. They aren't just phones you can recharge. What made them come alive last time might not work now.'

'Are you saying you don't know how to do it?'

'I'm afraid I don't. Camelot keeps its own secrets. You're going to have to work it out for yourselves.'

'You made the bloody things,' Carter muttered, still showing his anger at the whole situation.

'I did, son. That doesn't mean I control them any more than I can tell you all what to do. You have free will. If you want, I can take you back to the flat. I won't ever come near you again, if that's what you want.'

'You know they don't,' growled Liz. 'They'll follow you from one lunatic adventure to the next until they've all been killed. You're the same as Madoc, really. You never know when to stop.'

'I'm sorry you think that, Liz. I really am.'

Luca moved between his mum and Ambrose.

'Stop it, both of you. We're not stupid. We know the risks. We know how this might end, but what's the alternative? Do we just let Madoc get away with what he did?'

'You've done more than enough already,' Liz said.

'They have,' agreed Ambrose, 'but there is plenty more to do yet. Madoc isn't giving up. Even now, he is searching for someone who can help him get what he wants.'

'Who?'

'A special girl. Someone I've watched for a while, and someone who now knows she's as involved in this as you are. If Madoc gets to her, he could unleash darker magic than the raven spell. I can't bear to imagine the consequences if he succeeds.'

'You're not making any sense!' Luca shouted. 'Just for once, tell us what we need to know!'

Ambrose smiled sadly.

'You're right. Half a story here, a bit of a riddle there. The way ahead used to be clear as the morning light, but now it's always shadows and dust.' He swivelled around to face Freddie. 'The Black Prince spoke through you. How did that happen?'

Before Freddie could answer, Jess pulled him away.

'Leave him alone.'

'It's a fair question,' Ambrose replied. 'Something allowed him to come alive. Young Freddie has that special gift, doesn't he? He can read minds and hear thoughts. Trouble is, the same gift let the Black Prince find a way back from the prison that has held him for more than six hundred years and that is a serious problem. Madoc is planning to use a spell that could bring the Prince back to life. By accident, Freddie has made it more likely he will succeed. Madoc still has my spell book. The damned thing is more trouble than its worth. It can't be destroyed and it will always return to its master. The ravens have picked up chatter among the criminal community. Word is, there's a search going on for an old woman who disappeared a long time ago.

They won't find her. She's dead. They might, however, find her granddaughter.'

'The girl you just mentioned,' Liz said.

'Yes. She knows how to unlock the dark magic that Madoc wants to use. If he can force her to do it, the Black Prince could live again. He's already seen the world through Freddie's eyes. Imagine if he gets the chance to escape.'

'What would happen if he did? He would be a ghost, or something?'

'No! He would be real. It was said that the Plantagenets had the blood of the devil in them. The Prince will be changed by centuries in the grip of dark magic. If someone tastes a drop of his blood they can use that magic to become king. Madoc knows that. He has to be stopped. You must find a way to waken the swords and you must get to this girl. Protect her from Madoc at any cost.'

He clicked his fingers and Bran flew up onto his shoulder.

'Go to the Tower, Bran. Bring Madeleine. Yes, her uncle too. I will bring the other one.'

Bran spiralled up into the vast darkness above their heads, each graceful flap lifting him higher until he disappeared.

'I must leave you again.'

'To bring the other one, you said. Who is that?'

'You'll see.'

Luca studied his face - old and lined but with young eyes. Full of fear and desire in equal measure.

'You're enjoying this,' Luca said.

'Yes. I can't deny that. What else do I have if I have don't have this?'

'I don't know you. I never knew you as Peake. You just come and go. Like my dad.'

'No, Luca. He was there for you and he has never left you.' Ambrose touched Luca's chest. 'He's in there, always. Never forget that.'

'Is that it?'

But Ambrose did not reply, and the silence said everything. He closed his eyes, clicked his fingers and disappeared.

'So,' Carter said, 'you know that plan where we find somewhere quiet to hide?'

'Not gonna happen,' Luca replied.

'Thought so. Come on, then. Let's get into Camelot.'

But before any of them could move, from high up in the echoing dizzy heights of the cavern roof, they heard the ravens returning.

'Here they come,' Freddie said.

Two shapes were just visible among the birds, one large and struggling, the other much smaller and seemingly floating along like a paper boat on a stream. Madeleine was singing and laughing. McKenna was definitely not doing either. His voice was a long high-pitched scream of terror that bounced off the cavern walls in a ghostly echo.

'He's not enjoying the ride,' said Freddie. 'Shame. I think it's great fun.'

The ravens swooped around them, beaks and claws scratching mischievously across their skin and tugging at their hair. They landed in great piles on the sand and moved apart like a wave rippling towards a shore. Two tangled bodies separated into arms and legs and heads, crawling to their feet as if they had just been thrown around the world's maddest roller coaster.

'Don't ever, ever, ever, let that happen to me again,' shouted McKenna, followed by a few swear words.

Madeleine hugged her uncle and laughed.

'Silly uncle Sam,' she said, holding up her favourite cuddly toy. 'It was lots of fun. In fact, I want to do it again and so does Hug-a-Bug!'

McKenna groaned and covered his eyes. He was shaking, more like a frightened child than a big tough soldier. 'And what exactly did just happen?'

'You were carried all the way from London by thousands of ravens,' Freddie stated, in a very Freddie kind of way. 'They lifted you across seventeen miles of freezing sea and propelled you through a tiny crack in the rocks before dropping you onto this beach next to Camelot. And like Madeleine said, it was lots of fun.'

'That's not the first word banging around my head,' McKenna groaned. His eyes widened as he took in the view. 'What the...'

McKenna couldn't take his eyes off the cliffs and lake, the statues and walls of the castle. His mouth was open and he kept shaking his head, as if he was expecting to wake up and find it had all been a crazy dream.

'All real,' Luca called to him. 'Mad, isn't it?'

The Ravenmaster nodded.

'Gets madder, I promise.'

'I was just about to enjoy a nice glass of wine when the ravens started going ballistic, all screaming and jumping around. I couldn't calm 'em down. Then guess what, thousands of their mates turn up and before I knew what was happening, me and Madeleine are up in the air like bloody Dorothy on her way to Oz.'

McKenna was babbling away, hardly stopping to take a breath,

'We know,' said Freddie. 'And we've done it ourselves. No big deal.'

McKenna didn't seem to have heard him. He was still recounting the journey, shaking his head, wiping his forehead, checking his limbs as if he might have left one of them behind. Eventually, he seemed to run out of things to say, and he stared at them as if he just seeing them for the first time.

'And you're all here. And you don't seem surprised to see us. Which means...'

'Yep,' said Luca, 'It's game on again. Madoc's back.'

Luca spoke quickly, bringing McKenna up to speed on what had happened and what they knew.

'So we, or you, have got to find a way to get your swords working again, and then save some kid who can raise the royal dead from being used by Madoc to do exactly that? Damn, I thought the last time was strange enough.'

Nobody spoke. Luca shrugged. His mum stepped forwards and held out a hand. McKenna took it gently.

'Liz Broom.'

'A pleasure. Sam McKenna. I've heard a lot about you from your son, Liz. And as an old soldier, I'm sorry for the loss of your husband.'

'Thank you. It was a long time ago.'

'And I bet it feels like yesterday.'

Luca noticed a faint flush of red across his mum's throat, and the way McKenna held her hand for a few more seconds before letting go. Then the moment passed and the two of them coughed and looked away. Carter nudged him in the ribs and winked.

'Come on,' he shouted. 'Let's get on with this.'

They started walking towards the statues. As they passed by, the huge stone knights raised their swords in greeting. McKenna and Liz didn't say a word. It was just another unbelievable thing to take in. They reached the archway and door that led into Camelot,

They passed under the zodiac carving. Luca reached up and touched the stone. It was surprisingly warm, like summer skin. Then he noticed how splintered the door was, pock-marked by bullet holes.

'I was left behind here,' Freddie said, his voice ringing out like a mournful bell, cutting through the chatter of the birds. 'I didn't think I was going to survive.'

Was that really how Freddie thought it had been? Luca could only remember chaos and terror, and gunfire and smoke. Each one of them had been a second from capture or death.

'We didn't know what was going on,' Luca said. 'Honest, Freddie. I'm sorry, mate. I really am.'

'It's okay,' Freddie replied. 'It all worked out in the end.'

Did it? Luca thought. I'm not so sure.

There was something dark behind Freddie's eyes that he couldn't quite work out, but after hearing what Ambrose had to say, Luca could guess it was something to do with the Black Prince.

10

Freya moved silently through the windmill. She touched the pistol at her hip and carried on checking the traps. They were old and rusty but they still worked. She tested one with a stick, prodding at the heavy iron teeth until they clamped down. The satisfying crunch and the skittering of splinters told her all she needed to know. Tread on one and your foot would be smashed in a dozen painful places. Freya climbed up the stairs and surveyed the scene below. Twenty of the lethal traps were scattered across the floor, from the barricaded front door to the bottom of the stairs, like a mass of crabs waiting to attack.

An hour later, after a quick tea of beans on toast, Freya settled in the armchair. She stared at a small picture frame that she had placed directly in front of her. The frame was darkened silver. The photograph was stained around the edges by years of damp. Freya wanted to look away but she couldn't. It had been so many years since the photograph had been on display. Her mum didn't like it, understandably.

I miss you both.

And the thought was like a punch in the stomach as she looked at her parents smiling out from the photograph, her dad holding her up to the camera. She was grinning the way toddlers do. Her mum looked happier than anybody could ever dare to hope they would be. Her dad, so handsome in his Army uniform, was bursting with pride.

'And then you left us,' she whispered. 'Because of who I am.'

He had been there a few times for the first couple of years. Random weekends, sometimes longer, and the one unforgettable summer when they went to Southend for a few days - ice creams and sandcastles and sunburn soothed by his gentle voice. She didn't know at the time it was his way of saying goodbye. The Army sent him overseas and they lost touch. Then last year, the special time that she played over and over in her mind, when out of the blue he contacted her.

Her mum hadn't wanted her to go, because she was still so angry with him even after so long, but Freya needed to hear him explain why he had felt he had no choice but to leave his wife and only child. She had gone up to the Tower and been completely overwhelmed by the high walls and the frowning soldiers with guns, and the ravens with eyes like drops of blood and curved beaks ready to rip at her. Their cries had reached into her soul and Freya knew the birds were scared of her, because of who and what she was, and she had wanted to go home to her mum but wanted more to stay with her dad in that incredible place where he was a Yeoman Warder, a guardian of the Tower and the kingdom - one of the select few. But he was, more than anything else, her dad, and she had missed him more than anything she could ever imagine.

More than I miss mum, she thought.

And as soon as she had thought it, the pain of guilt was like a physical thing.

'I'm sorry,' she said, to the empty room.

Freya looked at the calendar, with its thick black crosses through each of the days since her mum had driven off, ignoring Freya's pleading to take her too, but there had been no chance of that. Her mum was ill and did what she thought was best – get away, look for help. And the last few days weren't crossed off, because after this long without any contact, Freya knew her mum had gone away to die, so what was the point?

And what about her dad - was he out there somewhere wondering about her? Maybe he was dead. Or maybe he didn't really care.

Except in her heart she knew that couldn't be true.

'So I wait here,' she said angrily as she moved away from the photograph. She didn't need to look at it now. She needed to be focused and strong for what was coming. Ambrose had been very specific on that, even as she cursed him for coming into her home and telling her things she didn't want to hear. She didn't want any part of his madness but there was no way to escape his silent smile and those bright eyes, somehow young and ancient at the same time. And of course, the raven on his shoulder had fixed her with the deepest of stares and reached into her mind, whispering to her in a language that she could understand without any idea how.

This was the thing she had always known would happen, ever since she was a little girl and her mum had whispered to her of their wonderful family secret, the magical gift Freya had inherited from her dad's mother.

Over the years, she had tried to remember that first conversation and how different her life would have been if she had not listened, or had run outside to play, or done any one of a hundred other things to show her mum she wasn't interested, but of course there was no escaping it. All of the times she had been shown the magic by her nan, all of the times she had been told who and what she was, all of the times they had spoken to each other without words, and it had never crossed her mind that if her dad found out he would actually leave. How could that even have happened? Why was the magic such a bad thing? Was he really that scared of his own flesh and blood?

She couldn't stop herself from glancing back at the photograph. His smile was wide. He held her so high. Suddenly, unexpectedly, she started to cry. She wiped away the years with an angry growl. No way. Not any more. Her crying days were done. She was thirteen and alone but that was just fine. It would have to be.

'I never asked to be a witch,' she said, 'and neither did nan. It's just what it is.'

She checked her watch. Outside, the light was fading and the wind had picked up. Maybe this evening would be the one that the men came looking for her, or maybe not. Either way, she would be ready for them when they did. She would not sleep. She was done with dreaming. The gun was no longer at her hip. It was in her hand.

11

Every step took them deeper into the tunnels and passages of the castle. Luca knew they had totally failed to remember which way they had gone the last time, when they were escaping Madoc's men. Every door looked the same. Every metre of tunnel was identical. It didn't matter how many times they stopped and argued whether it was left or right at this junction or that. Each decision was wrong. The walls were damp down here, and cold, and they glowed pale green as they walked past, lit by some strange unnatural power. At one point they had to move in single file because it was so narrow. At another point the tunnel seemed to stretch above them forever. Luca had the distinct feeling they were going around in circles, and McKenna started scratching on the walls with the tip of his penknife just in case they were, but they never saw the marks again, so at least they knew they were heading somewhere. All the time that green light floated around them like a sunrise that never quite happened.

'I would say we're definitely lost,' McKenna said, and just as he did so a ghostly shape appeared from the darkest shadows. They either jumped or screamed, or both, but the shape coalesced into a man dressed in chain mail and sword. His clothing was old and tattered and he shone like silver.

They backed up, ready to run or fight. The knight studied them. He tilted his head one way then the other, like a scientist examining some bugs under a microscope. He rubbed his chin. Then he held up a hand in greeting.

'You can see me? You really can? Oh, that is most wonderful!'

Nobody replied. The knight tried again.

'I heard you approach from a long way away. You really are most noisy. Who are you?'

Still no reaction from his stunned audience.

'Do you speak English? Are you all stupid?'

'Yeah,' Luca replied, deciding one of them had to say something. 'I mean, we speak English. Not the stupid bit.'

'Good. I thought for a moment you might all be idiots.'

He approached them, hand on his sword.

'Watch it,' whispered Carter. 'If he tries anything, jump him.'

The knight looked at Carter.

'You're a spirited fellow. Do you have the fight to match?'

'You bet,' and Carter was certainly ready, dancing on the balls of his feet, fists up.

The knight laughed and took his hand away.

'Well said, young man. Well said. Let's not dwell on such things. We should, in fact, be more interested in talking than fighting, because it can be a very difficult thing to fight a ghost.'

And then he pushed his hand into the tunnel wall. It disappeared, then reappeared, and his trick had the desired effect. They stepped even further back. The ghostly knight just laughed.

'I'm sorry. A poor attempt at humour.'

In spite of him being a ghost, which was strange enough, and the odd way he spoke, or perhaps because of it, Luca immediately liked him and he might show them the way to the Great Hall. That was the best plan they had. Get there and see if the table would fix the swords, in spite of what Ambrose had said.

'We're not here to cause any trouble,' Luca said. 'You just surprised us, that's all.'

'I expect I am somewhat surprising.'

'Meeting a ghost? Yeah, not happened to us before.'

'Of course.'

The knight lifted off the floor, hovering in the air. He faded away, becoming almost transparent, but his eyes remained like two glowing jewels. Then the fade ended. He was more solid again. The knight looked down at his suspended feet and he laughed, as if the sight of what he could do was the funniest thing he had ever seen.

'Such things still amuse me, even after all these years,' he said as he floated back to earth, but even then his feet didn't really make contact with the corridor floor. They seemed to drift against it, almost like mist over a dawn lake. 'This is all very exciting. I haven't had guests at Camelot for so long. It does get rather lonely, wandering around talking to the spiders and the rats. Have you ever tried striking up a meaningful conversation with a rat?'

They all shook their heads.

'I expect not. And you, my lady. You are the mother of this fine young knight?'

Liz said she was, and the ghost paused, as if waiting for her to say more, but when she didn't he smiled and drifted on, still chatting away.

'Yes, very exciting. And what has brought you here, in your strange clothes the like of which I have never seen before?'

Luca glanced at the others, trying to decide how best to play this. He pushed away the fact he was talking to a ghost. Nothing was normal any more, and this was just something else to get his head around. The most important thing was whether they could trust him. He seemed friendly enough, and was clearly pleased to have them there, so maybe there was no harm in telling him.

'Be careful,' Jess whispered.

Luca could tell she wasn't completely sure. Freddie didn't seem bothered either way. Gwen said nothing and Carter looked like...well, he looked like Carter, ready for a fight regardless of whether he needed to or not.

'Go easy,' McKenna said.

'Hug-a-Bug is scared,' added Madeleine, gripping the ladybird even more tightly than normal

They couldn't just stand there forever, so Luca decided to see if the knight could help them.

'We were brought here by the ravens,' he said, choosing his words carefully.

'I see. They had a reason, I would imagine.'

'Yeah. Because of who we are.'

Now the knight seemed to tense, if it was possible for a ghostly shadow to do that.

'We've got swords,' Luca said, and lifted his up for the knight to see.

The knight closed the gap to Luca in a second. He peered at the sword. He raised a hand as if to touch it, but his hand fell away. He took a long, deep, ghostly breath.

'All of you?'

'Not my mum. Or him.' Luca nodded at McKenna. 'The rest of us, yeah.'

The ghost shimmered and glowed, faded and reappeared again. He gasped and laughed, hugging himself like a child on Christmas morning.

'Sword bearers here at Camelot? How extraordinary! I watched Arthur's knights carry those swords away from here after that terrible battle. I called and shouted at them but I was already more ghost than man. They couldn't see or hear me. Now the swords are back. Oh, my word, this really is the most wonderful of days. The most wonderful!'

He rose up to the roof of the tunnel, singing some strange tuneless song in a language that Luca didn't recognise. He floated down again, collecting himself. He bowed deeply, and his feet lifted up behind him so that his forehead almost brushed the floor.

'You don't need to do that,' Luca said, embarrassed. 'We're only here because Peake brought us. I mean Ambrose. Or Merlin.'

The knight froze. He nearly faded away to nothing and a quiet choking noise came from his ghostly throat.

'You all right?' Luca asked.

'Merlin, here?'

The knight reappeared, like a rabbit carefully checking out if there was a stoat ready to pounce.

'Not here. Not in the castle. Out there, by the lake. Actually, he's gone now. Why does it matter?'

The knight crossed himself and muttered a short prayer.

'Good.'

'You don't like him?'

'It matters not whether I like him. I fear him. Too strange. Too strange.'

'He can be strange, but I don't think you need to be scared of him.'

'Well,' the knight said, 'that is where you and I may disagree.'

'Are you one of the knights of the Round Table?'

The ghost looked down.

'No, sir. I was never good enough to sit there with the chosen ones. I was just a nameless faceless soldier guarding the Arthur's castle, but I did a good job. We all did. Until that day when Mordred brought his army of painted devils. That day, there was nothing any of us could do. Not even the king.'

'You died in that battle?'

'I did. And then I woke up like this, and I have wandered the tunnels and passages ever since.' He kicked out at a pebble with a non-existent foot, and then cursed when it passed straight through. 'See? What am I but a cloud? A memory of the man I was, and all because of that wizard.'

Then he began to cry, and it was the saddest most desolate sound that Luca had ever heard. A thousand years of misery let loose in that dark, damp tunnel.

'Why do you blame Peake?' Carter asked. 'I mean Ambrose. Oh, bloody hell, Merlin or whatever he's called.'

'Because he could have saved us all but he did nothing.'

'He told us he turned Mordred into thousands of beetles and they were all eaten by the ravens.'

'Did he?' The knight didn't look that interested. 'I must have already been dead on the ground by then.'

'So why you? As a ghost, I mean? What about all the others who died?'

The knight's face changed. His eyes narrowed.

'I was the only knight that directly challenged Mordred. His sword passed through me and I felt the awful chill of its dark magic. And ever since, I have remained here, alone.'

'I'm really sorry,' Luca said, and he meant it.

The knight lifted his face. The tears welled up and evaporated away into nothing, because they were no more solid than his eyes.

'Not as sorry as me, young knight. Not as sorry as I have been every day since.'

'This is terrible,' whispered Jess. 'Poor man. What can we do?'

'I don't think we can do anything,' Freddie said.

'No, you cannot.'

The knight wiped a transparent hand across his equally transparent eyes, sniffed and straightened up.

'Forgive me. It was the mention of the wizard. It took me back. So why did he bring you here? What has happened?'

They looked at each other. There didn't seem to be any reason not to tell him.

'It's like this,' Luca began, and then he ran through everything. The knight listened intently. He gasped when Luca explained who Gwen was. He didn't speak at all, not even when Luca finished. They stood in awkward silence.

'Well?' Luca asked at last. 'Now you know everything.'

'I do. And your swords are cold. Dead. Lifeless. Rather like me.' He laughed thinly at his own joke. 'I can help you,' he said. 'Perhaps this has been my fate, to wait here for sword bearers to return. You see, I may know how you can wake the swords.'

They all spoke at once, questions merging into one.

The knight held up his hands for them to be quiet.

'This way. I will show you what you have to do.'

He headed away from them at speed and there was little choice but to follow. The tunnel narrowed and again they had to scramble along in single file. All the time they were moving downhill. Luca tried to imagine how far underground they were, but it was impossible, and the thought of it wasn't pleasant. There was so much rock above them. The smallest shift, the tiniest nudge, and it all might come crashing down.

Luca thought he heard running water up ahead, and as they kept moving the sound filled the tunnel and the air became damp. They wiped the moisture from their faces and hair, and it was suddenly too hot. Luca stripped off his coat. Breathing was hard work. The knight had merged into the mist, except for his glinting eyes whenever he turned back to check they were still following. Suddenly the mist cleared for a second and the knight floated closer.

'There you are, my friends.'

His hand swept through the mist, clearing it even more, and Luca wished he hadn't.

The path ended abruptly. After that was a vast chasm maybe fifty metres across. Seven flat topped stone columns rose up from the darkness, and each one seemed tantalisingly close, but Luca could see it was a hell of a jump from one to the next. He chanced a look over the edge. He couldn't see anything through the mist. It made his head swim to imagine how far the fall might be.

'A long way,' whispered Freddie, in his head.

'Thanks. That really helps.'

'You're welcome.'

The knight floated out over the abyss. He hung in the air like a balloon losing its helium, not light enough to rise but not yet dense enough to give in to gravity, then he drifted back to them.

'There you are.'

He pointed at the other side of the chasm, where a thin white light in the shape of a sword had appeared. In no time, the light shone brightly over the columns, casting deep shadows into the mist.

'All you have to do is cross.'

With that, he bowed once more and vanished.

12

The narrow cobbled streets of Canterbury were more like shadowy tunnels, barely lit by the occasional working light. Snow drifted out of a slate grey sky onto the cobbles and turned them into a slippery assault course ready to break an ankle or wrist. A mean wind whistled through the place. A few people scurried along, heads down against the cold, all eager to be back inside. The place felt unstable, somehow. Without the hustle and bustle of shoppers and the welcoming glow and warmth of the shops and coffee houses, Canterbury was like a city of a previous age, where darkness was a thief's best friend and the cold was something for everybody to fear.

Just off the main thoroughfare, close to the cathedral precinct, stood the King's School. The pupils had been moved to Scotland as soon as the plague started to spread out from London, but it had been a calm evacuation and now they were safely back as if nothing had ever happened. School continued as it had done for centuries. Quiet. Unfussy. Unstoppable.

A small crowd of boys had gathered outside, their faces turned up to the sky. On such a short day, any light was welcome, but the day was nearly done and the snow was turning to sleet. One boy stood apart from the rest. Tall, slim, hands stuffed into the pockets of his trousers, his gaze was fixed on something entirely different.

There it is again, George Randall thought.

The object of his gaze lifted up from the skeletal branches of a tree just outside the sodden school walls, flapped its enormous black wings and disappeared into the gathering gloom, calling as it went. A shiver ran down George's spine. He had never heard anything as eerie as that lonely echoing cry.

'What are you staring at, Randall?' shouted a boy called Woods.

George ignored the question, and the boy who had asked it. In fact, he planned on ignoring all of them for the rest of the day, just as he had done for most of his time in Canterbury. He had always felt different. Recently, for no reason he could explain, that feeling had changed. George searched for the right word.

Special, he thought. That's how I feel.

The thought popped into his head like that odd dream he had been having – the one where a red haired girl stood on the ramparts of a castle and smiled at him, whilst huge black birds swirled around her. She was his age but somehow younger. He could never quite make out her face, because of the birds. They weren't regular crows. They were bigger with chunky beaks and intelligent eyes. He guessed they were ravens. They always got in the way of the girl, like a washing line of greasy black cloths. Then she would fade away as he woke. He had searched online for her, but he had no idea where to start.

This new thought was the same; only a faint smudge of something that he should understand but just too far away to grab hold of. Special. What did that even mean? And that bird kept coming to the school, and it was definitely a raven...

'I said, what are you staring at? You must be deaf as well as stupid.'

George turned slowly, like oil sliding along a glass tube. A small crowd had gathered around Woods, sensing action.

'Maybe,' George said. 'Maybe not, but because you're thicker than anybody, you'll never be able to work out the difference.'

The punch caught him on the tip of the nose, and it caused immediate tears. George fought the urge to blink. The pain was like a burning knife, but he could handle that. It was the shame that really dug into him, because deep down he knew he had asked for it. A ragged cheer rippled through the crowd.

'You're pathetic,' Woods sneered.'

George held his breath. He wanted to fight back, but he had nothing – neither strong blows nor clever words. He stood like a statue. Woods shook his head in disgust. George's eyes dropped to the floor. His head buzzed with the chatter of the popular kids that milled around him on their way to stuff their faces. He could hear them making fun of him but he didn't turn around or respond. Woods had got to him. And maybe Woods was right – he wasn't special, he was pathetic.

He slunk away from the scene of his most recent humiliation and headed to his room. He leaned against the door and flipped the lock. He looked around the spartan space – just a bed and a desk, a small lamp, a mirror. No posters, no bright duvet cover. Nothing to mark it out as his. Just a few books on a shelf and a rucksack stuffed under the bed. He could be packed and gone in five minutes.

And nobody would even notice, he thought. Just because I don't have loads of money. Just because my parents are dead. Just because I'm not one of the in-crowd.

He could hear Woods shouting insults from down below, and George wondered how long that might last. The record so far was an hour. At least he was indoors and dry while that idiot was out there in the freezing sleet.

Then the shouting stopped. Something tapped on his window. George jumped up, startled. How could that be? His room was two floors up. Another tap, then another.

'What?'

The raven was sat on the window ledge, tapping away. George didn't move. He was too surprised to do anything. The raven tapped harder. The glass cracked. One more tap and the glass shattered. Pieces flew across the room like daggers. Then the raven hopped onto his bed.

George looked from bird to window and back to bird, scarcely able to believe what was happening.

Special.

Had the raven just spoken to him? No. That was insane. Birds can't speak.

Special. Special. Special.

And then he realised he could hear the raven in his head.

'So that's okay, then,' George laughed nervously.

He was stood in his bedroom with a telepathic bird.

'I hope you're going to pay for that window,' he said, because he didn't know what else to say.

The raven tilted his head and seemed to smile, if that was something a raven could do. Then it stumbled awkwardly over his duvet and jumped up onto George's shoulder. His knees buckled under the weight and he grabbed the back of the chair just in time to stop him falling. The raven pecked at his hair.

'Get off!'

The raven clearly had no intention of doing that. In fact, the pecking turned into pulling. George had no choice but to move the way the raven wanted him to go, which was towards the window. For a moment, George thought the bird was going to pull him through it, and that would be a quick way to get his throat cut, but instead his head was steered around until he was looking down at Woods. He was completely still, almost as if frozen in the moment, and then George saw another figure emerge from the shadows.

'What the hell is going on?' he asked, but got no reply from the raven pulling on his hair. Instead, the figure stepped out so he could be seen more clearly, and George realised two things at the same moment. Firstly, he recognised the man who was looking up at him.

You were outside school the other week, he thought. I spoke to you. You said your name was Ambrose.

And secondly, he understood that Woods was standing still as a statue because that was exactly what he seemed to have become. George shoved open the door and flew down the stairs three at a time, followed by a very agitated raven that was doing its best to keep up with him. He shrugged the bird away as he skidded over to where Woods stood motionless, his eyes half open as if trapped in mid-blink. His mouth was slack at the corners.

'Hello, again,' Ambrose said, completely untroubled.

The raven landed by his feet and cackled incessantly until the man raised a finger to his lips. The raven fell silent. It preened its feathers and glared at George.

'Who...what...what have you done to him?'

'He's fine, I assure you. Just asleep. Well, sort of asleep.'

'This isn't real,' he said. 'I must have been knocked out by his punch. This is all a dream.'

'It most definitely is real. That punch was little more than a tap.'

'You were there?'

'I'm everywhere, George. Everywhere and always.'

It was suddenly much colder. The raven clicked softly and Ambrose paused to listen. More clicks and whistles, croaks and clacks.

'I know,' Ambrose nodded. 'We're just about to go.'

'Go where? Talk to me, you lunatic, not the weird chicken down there.'

'That's quite funny. His name is Bran, by the way. And this unpleasant child will wake up the second after we disappear. I promise.'

'Disappear?'

'Yes. You and me and the chicken.'

Ambrose laughed and moved closer. George raised his fists.

'I'm not going to hurt you, George. And as we've already seen, fighting's not your thing.'

Ambrose touched George's sleeve. Everything started to go grey and a sudden surge of nausea rushed through his gut. He staggered backwards. The school buildings broke up and faded away, and George felt himself dropping and spinning and disappearing.

13

'Well, that's just great.' Carter asked.

Luca slumped down onto the floor. It had been a mistake to follow the ghost. Now they were so far from where they had started, he doubted they could ever find their way back. And to jump across? He took another look over the edge. His stomach flipped.

'No real Plan B,' said McKenna, staring across the rock columns.

Eight jumps and each one likely to be the last. How could anybody stand there and contemplate it?

No choice, Luca thought.

'Plan A, then. We get across.'

The shining sword was so bright he couldn't look directly at it, and the glow from each of the smaller swords made it clear that was what they had to do.

Luca took a deep breath. This whole Pendragon thing was seriously hard work. He knew the others were waiting on him. He studied the nearest column. Flat and round, big enough probably for three of them if they spread out. The sides disappeared into the mist. Fall off and you might still be tumbling a week later. Or forever.

'Reckon you can make it?' Carter whispered.

'Can you?'

'I will if you will.'

'But we've got to, yeah?'

'Yeah.'

Luca guessed that he could make the first stone with a decent run up even though his brain was firing off like a rocket, screaming not to do it.

'Just jump,' said Freddie, straight to the point as always. 'I'm sure you won't fall. If you do, it'll be over in no time.'

'Thanks,' Luca replied. 'That's very helpful.'

'Any time.'

Luca tried to work out who might be wavering. Carter was unusually quiet, clearly aware this was serious stuff. Gwen the same. Jess looked calm, but then she always did. Madeleine was huddled between his mum and McKenna, her face hidden behind Hug-a-Bug. Freddie just smiled at him.

'You'll jump, won't you?' he asked.

'Of course,' Freddie replied, still smiling. 'Where else am I going?'

'Fair enough. Me first, then. Decide between you who goes next. And if anybody really doesn't want to do it, that's okay.'

Maybe we could find another way across, Liz said.

'Luca's right,' McKenna replied. 'This is Plan A through to Z. We'd never find our way back to the lake and even if we did, what does that achieve. Whichever way we go, I suspect we'd end up back here.'

'It's completely suicidal,' she argued. 'And what about Madeleine? Do you really believe she can make it?'

'Why not? McKenna replied. 'Are you saying because she has Down's syndrome she's not as good as the others?'

'No, of course not. I'm just pointing out how dangerous it is. You know I'm right.'

'If Freddie goes, so will I,' Madeleine said in a tiny voice.

'Decision made,' said Freddie. 'Get on with it, Luca.'

And just like that, Luca prepared to jump. He breathed deeply, in and out, swinging his arms and rocking on his toes, trying to judge the distance and where he would land. The stone's surface glistened with condensation and that was worrying. It would be so easy to slide straight off the other side. Well, as Freddie had said, it would be over quickly if that happened.

He counted silently down from ten, hands clenched, eyes focused on the stone. Six, five, four, three, two, one...

'Go!'

His legs cycled and his arms swung forwards. He was tumbling out over the edge and then he landed squarely, but the surface was even more slippery than he had feared and he slid towards the far side. One more step and he would go over. He swayed over the precipice for a moment, his heart almost stopping with terror, but he pulled himself back, gasping for breath.

'Easy,' he shouted, very aware he had made it look anything but that.

The next stone was closer, and slightly below him, which made the jump a whole lot easier. He landed better and was able to stop a decent distance from the edge. He was already soaked through by the mist and he wiped his face and hair. He blinked to clear his vision and jumped again, not stopping to think. Another solid landing. He jumped again. And again. Four down. Four to go.

He turned to look at the others but they were obscured by the disturbed mist. Their faces were no more than pale blobs.

'I'm okay,' he shouted.

'Be careful,' his mum shouted, as if he wasn't already.

The next stone wasn't level. A ridge ran across the middle at an awkward angle, so an unlucky landing might turn his ankle or worse. It looked to be the longest jump yet. Luca launched himself across, and he was moving slower than he should have been.

Falling's okay, he thought. It's the stopping I don't like.

That made him laugh out loud even as he pitched forwards towards the ugly uneven surface of the column. Then he landed, knees banging hard against the ridge. His hands scraped over the rock. He just managed to roll onto his side, avoiding the face-plant that would have sandpapered his nose and forehead.

His bullet scar throbbed painfully but after a quick count to ten Luca climbed to his feet.

He gauged the next jump. Comparatively easy, not too far and a wide landing area. He went for it before he had too much time to decide otherwise. One jump to go. And then the mist cleared, and his heart sank. There was no way of getting across to the other side. The gap was massive. It was as if a stone was missing between him and safety.

I need you, Bran, he thought.

It would be so easy if a few ravens were there to lift him across.

'Where are you when I really need you?'

His voice echoed across the chasm and he looked back the way he had come. He suddenly realised something – all of the jumps had been slightly down, meaning that to go back was impossible. There was just no way he could get enough height.

I'm stuck. No way forwards and no way back.

Luca lay down, his cheek pressed against the cold stone. The world was suddenly no more than the narrow horizontal view of mist and unreachable rock. He closed his eyes. He tried to ignore the pain in his leg but it pulsed like a stopwatch counting down to the end of it all.

He thought of his dad, and how he would have handled this. What would he have done?

Maximum danger.

'What?'

The thought had landed in his head like an avalanche. It meant something. He searched for it, the memory just out of reach.

'What does that even mean?'

Then he remembered. Something he had seen on YouTube. Who was it, parachuting?

'Will Smith,' he said out loud.

That was it. The actor, telling an audience what he had felt as he stood in the door of a plane, ready to jump.

The point of maximum danger is the point of minimum fear.

And Luca completely understood what it meant. There was now, and there was the rest of forever. The mist was so thick now, he could hardly see his fingers when he held them up. The light was odd, almost white and milky. The edge of the stone blurred into the mist, and he imagined for a second that he could walk out onto it, simple as that.

Luca sat up. He stared across the mist and as his vision became tuned in to the swirling vapour, he saw something so incredible, he didn't really believe it was actually there.

'Is that even possible?' he whispered.

He took a deep breath, climbed to his feet and edged towards the edge of the stone. His toes pressed down into his shoes. He locked his knees. He balanced himself.

'One way to find out. Maximum danger, here we go.'

Then he stepped out into nothing.

14

Madoc sipped his tea, comfortable in the armchair, enjoying the heat from the log burner. He liked this house, with its large bay windows and soft ticking clocks. The wood smoke reminded him of his childhood and visits to his grandfather's home overlooking the Atlantic ocean. There had always been a fire in the the hearth to dry away the salt spray that never seemed to relent even in the middle of summer. That part of Ireland was wild and untamed, just like the old man who had made it his home. Madoc loved him as much as he was scared of him. He would sit Madoc down and question him on every aspect of his life, challenging him on what he would achieve and how he would do it, and make him promise over and over that he would never give up the dream of restoring the family to where it rightfully should be. And Madoc would do his best to give the answers his grandfather wanted to hear.

'I've never stopped trying, sir,' he whispered now as he looked out at the city below. 'I've failed you so far, but this time will be different. The Devil's blood is the way to get what we both wanted.'

Gabriel knocked softly before entering.

'Johnson will be here soon. He texted me to say he has news. And I've made contact with one of your team in Canterbury. Eyes on the ground, looking for your daughter or the others.'

'There's always someone willing to help me, eh? That's the smell of money, you know.'

'Yes, sir. I've not had any news since that incident in Winchester. They could be anywhere.'

'They could be, but don't concern yourself with it. Merlin is back and he'll send his pathetic little army of children to try and stop me again. If he guesses what I'm going to do, he'll get them to Canterbury. Which is fine, because we'll be ready for them. In fact, I need them to be there.'

Just then, the doorbell rang. Gabriel motioned for Madoc to hide. He pulled out a pistol and moved to the door. Madoc breathed slowly behind the curtains, hating what he had become, struggling to control his impatience. He was desperate to get on with the next stage of the plan but until he had the girl he just had to wait.

'It's him.'

'Is he alone?'

'Yes.'

'No girl, then.'

'I'll bring him through.'

'You do that.'

Johnson looked tired, and nervous. He kept glancing out of the window and at Gabriel. Madoc let him sweat for a while. Finally, he pointed at one of the armchairs. Johnson took the hint and sank down.

'I had rather hoped you might be here with someone else. You know, the person you're supposed to be finding.'

'She'll be yours very soon. My men have definitely identified the girl and where she lives. It's an old windmill out on Dungeness marsh. Absolute back of nowhere. They're headed there now.'

'Good. As soon as they have her, I want to know.'

'I've got more to tell you. Report of an odd incident in Winchester. Bunch of kids matching the description of your daughter and the others. Officers had them cornered but there was a flash of light and lots of ravens. And another massive raven disturbance at the Tower. Lots of birds flying west.'

'I already know this.' Madoc said.

'A man appeared from nowhere,' Johnson continued, trying to interest Madoc in his information. 'I've got a good description of him. Tall, angular, white hair. Distinguished looking, like a professor.'

'That's not the man I saw by the lake,' Gabriel said.

'He can change,' replied Madoc. 'He's done it before.'

Johnson looked utterly bemused but he had the sense to stay quiet.

'He's definitely taken them back to Camelot. I just know he has.'

'Then they're out of our way, sir.'

'Exactly what I was thinking.' Madoc turned to face Johnson. 'A good job, Commissioner. Please encourage your men to secure the girl.'

'What are you going to do to her?'

'Cold feet, Johnson? Worried you'll have more blood on your hands?'

'It's a fair question, Madoc. I haven't completely lost all sense of right and wrong.'

'I'm touched,' Madoc laughed. 'Don't worry. I very much need the girl alive.'

He thought of what was to come, in a secret place under Canterbury cathedral, and he laughed even more.

15

Luca tipped forwards. His heart lurched. A moment passed when there was nothing but the mist and the silent darkness, and a feeling that it was all over. Then his foot made contact with solid rock and he threw himself forwards, hugging the wet stone as if his life depended on it, which in many ways it did.

'I knew it,' he gasped, and he scrambled across to the other side. When his heart rate was back to something approaching normal, he looked back at what he had crossed.

The final stone pillar had been carved from the rock face. A thin sliver of rock connected the platform to it, but from nearly every angle it was virtually invisible. The mist had wafted across the surface leaving just a trace of glistening condensation. That was enough to hint that the gap was just an optical illusion, but only the bravest or craziest explorers would be willing to risk stepping out into nothing.

Luca stood up and wiped his hands on his trousers. The others were barely visible but he gave them a wave and the loudest shout he could manage, just in case. Nobody seemed to be following him across. He shouted again and he heard McKenna reply, asking if he was okay.

'Yeah. Wait there. I'm going to check what's up ahead then I'll come back and let you know.'

Luca picked up a handful of fine sand and scattered it over the rock, showing the way from the platform. The others would see it and know what to do. He headed towards a narrow split in the rock, passing under the glowing sword, hovering way above him and lighting his way. How it was lit was a mystery, but he didn't pause to try and work it out. He wanted to move quickly on and see what was ahead.

The split was just big enough to get through if he turned sideways and breathed in, but it quickly opened up into a wider chamber and then a long upwards sloping tunnel. A gentle orange light picked out a series of strange markings carved into the smooth walls. They looked like letters of an unknown alphabet but Luca had no idea what they could be telling him. Don't go on any further, perhaps? Instructions on what to do? Maybe the answers to all the questions that were rattling around his brain.

He pushed on for ten minutes, relieved that there weren't any junctions to confuse him. He had made enough decisions for one day. The light grew and faded, almost as if the tunnel was an artery of some huge dormant creature and the light was the heartbeat, and if that was even partially correct, the tunnel could be leading Luca to the heart.

The light changed slowly, growing more yellow. A soft noise washed over him. It sounded like the sea from a long way away, but without the intermittent crash of waves. Luca wondered if he should go back.

They should be doing this together, but he also wanted to know what was ahead. And, with each step, he wanted to be the first.

'I'm the Pendragon,' he whispered. 'I've got to be the bravest.'

Carter wouldn't be doubting himself, he thought. He would just hurry up the tunnel. And Gwen would, too. And Freddie. In fact, they all would.

That made up his mind. He would investigate as far as he could, see what it was all about, and then head back. Better that way than flapping around, hesitating and scared. The soft rushing sounds was suddenly louder. He had to know what it was.

He turned another corner, and then halted, stunned, eyes wide open, breath trapped in his throat. Right in front of him was a waterfall of liquid gold.

16

Gwen decided it was time to do something. Watching Luca cross had been tense beyond belief, and now it had been more than two hours since he had disappeared from sight.

This is hopeless, she thought. We're standing here like a bunch of stupid ducks waiting for some bread to be thrown.

Even Carter had gone quiet, and he never, ever, had nothing to say.

'I can't stand this,' she said. 'I'm going.'

That woke them up. She stayed silent as they argued among themselves, Carter and Freddie in favour of going, Jess unsure, the adults adamant they should stay. Gwen looked at Luca's mum, pinched with illness and worry, but still a kind and friendly face. For a moment, Gwen imagined her own mum here, and the pain was almost physical.

Luca's mum smiled at her. Gwen returned the smile.

I really like you, she thought.

'Why do you think we shouldn't?' Gwen asked her. 'You let Luca go.'

Liz shrugged.

'I'm his mum, Gwen. The job description says that I have to protect him from all danger, every day of his life. Trouble is, life doesn't work out like that. And the hardest bit of being a parent is knowing I have to let him make his own decisions, which sometimes means make his own mistakes.'

'You're here with him. That means everything in my book.'

'Thank you. I can't really imagine what you've been through.'

'I have all of you, now. That's enough for me. And I'm not waiting any more.'

'You're a very brave young woman. I wish I was half as brave.'

Gwen blushed but said nothing.

'Luca told you to stay,' interrupted McKenna, his face grim and business-like. 'Well, I'll give you my opinion for what it's worth. There's no way Liz and me can get across there anyway, which means it's down to you kids. You were brought here for a reason and this is probably it. And as much as my brain is screaming no, deep down I know that's the way it is.'

'As much it hurts me to say it, I think you're right,' said Liz, and McKenna took her hand without asking.

Gwen sensed fear in both of them, but there was also a new and deep connection there, and Gwen's eyes unexpectedly brimmed with tears. It was good to see other people finding someone they cared for.

'I'll stay right here until I know where else I have to be,' said Liz. 'I've lived with this madness since the day Peake appeared in my home and told me my son was the rightful heir to the throne of Britain. There you go. Try announcing that at parents' evening.'

Gwen laughed. It broke the solemn mood.

'Not sure I can make it,' she said, 'but only one way to find out. Carter?'

'Massive yes,' he replied. 'If Luca did it, I can do it.'

'Jess? Freddie?'

Two nods.

'That just leaves you, Madeleine. What do you think?'

Madeleine squeezed Hug-a-Bug. She frowned and glanced at her uncle. The Ravenmaster was still and silent, his face unreadable.

'I'm not very good at jumping,' she said. 'And it's a long way down.'

'You can stay here with me and Luca's mum,' McKenna replied. 'They'll come back and tell you all about it.'

'No,' Madeleine said. 'I don't think they will. I think that will be that. So I have to go. I'm one of the team, aren't I?'

She turned to Jess as she asked that question. Jess pulled her close.

'I think you're the most important one of all us. And we love you whatever.'

Freddie touched Madeleine's shoulder.

'I'll jump with you. If we hold hands, it'll be okay. And if not, we'll scream and shout all the way to the bottom. Might even be fun.'

'This is insane,' growled McKenna. 'I've changed my mind. Wait a bit longer.'

'Wait for what, uncle Sam?' Madeleine asked.

'I don't know, darlin'. I really don't know.'

And just like that, it was decided. Carter would go first, because he refused to let anybody go before him. Then Gwen, followed by Jess, and then Freddie and Madeleine would jump together. A moment of silence fell across them all, and sometimes silence can be the loudest sound anybody can ever imagine, and this was one of those times. Then Carter kissed Gwen's cheek, grinned at them all and jumped. No special goodbye or team speech. Just a swing of the arms, a flex of the legs. Almost effortless, as was the landing. See, the jump said. No problem. Easy. When you're ready.

He jumped again. Gwen counted to five and followed him. She braced for impact. It hurt more than she expected, and that wasn't so good. She stood up, winded, trying to look as normal as possible.

'No problem,' she said, but she heard the slight crack in her voice that meant otherwise.

'Yeah,' Carter answered from up ahead. He was off again, yelling himself across the next gap.

The second jump gave her confidence. She was out there, now, somewhere between the start and the end. She focused ahead, squinting against the light from the sword. Dread built in Gwen's chest like a shadow drifting across a graveyard. How had they all got themselves into this mess?

Jess jumped next. The landing was clean.

'Gwen, you need to keep going,' Jess said, as if she was talking to someone blocking a supermarket aisle.

Gwen went for it. Her knee banged down with a sickening crack and stars exploded across her vision. She bit down hard to block in the scream that was trying to get out. Her lungs wouldn't work. Everything was stuck. She thought she might lose consciousness but slowly the pain eased and she could see again. Carter stared at her.

'You okay? You nearly went over the edge.'

'Thanks for that.'

'Sorry.'

Behind her, Jess jumped again. She looked calmer than anybody should, considering what they were doing. Another jump. Another good landing.

Gwen tested her knee. It took her weight. There wasn't any choice. She had to jump either way. She did just that. Carter was across, shouting something about the last jump being easy, just a thin bridge to the other side, and that Luca had chucked some sand across for them to see it, which made no sense until she crossed herself and was standing under the glowing sword. She and Carter were swiftly joined by Jess. And that just left Freddie and Madeleine.

'She won't make it,' Gwen whispered.

'She might,' Carter replied. 'She has to.'

At that distance, Freddie's face was no more than a blobby mask, unreadable like a shop window dummy. He was suddenly running, and Madeleine with him, but she was already falling behind. He took off and she had no choice but to do the same. Gwen gasped. Time seemed to stand still. The mist swirled like a cloak. Freddie hit the column hard. Madeleine landed next to him. They stood up. Somehow, beyond all reason, they had completed the first jump.

Madeleine grinned and stuck two thumbs in the air. Freddie was more focused on the next jump. Jess shouted to him, telling him what he needed to do mixed in with words of encouragement and support. He didn't seem to be listening. He was coiled like a cat, ready to strike. He grabbed Madeleine's hand and jumped. She wasn't ready. Their hands scrambled to connect. The angle was too flat. She wasn't going to make it...

They landed heavily in a chaotic tangle of limbs and rising steam. Freddie scrambled to his feet, Madeleine less quickly. Her smile was gone. That landing had hurt.

'This is awful,' Gwen said. 'I never imagined anything like this.'

'We've done worse. They'll be okay.'

She couldn't believe how calm Carter sounded. She wanted to get back out there, do anything she could to help, carry Madeleine on her back if necessary, but there was nothing any of them could do but watch.

So they stood helplessly as Freddie somehow got Madeleine across until there was just one more jump to make. After that, it was a simple walk across the bridge. Madeleine grinned. She waved Hug-a-Bug and ran forwards.

'Wait for Freddie,' Jess shouted, but it was too late. Madeleine was going to jump by herself. She was too flat in the air. She was going to fall short, but by some miracle both feet made contact with the rock. It seemed she had done it, for a moment. Gwen was focused on the angle of her legs. They needed to be upright and strong, not buckled. Madeleine was toppling backwards, as if a giant hand was pressing her chest. A scream rose in Gwen's throat.

'No!'

Freddie jumped and bundled into Madeleine, stopping her fall and almost knocking himself over the edge at the same time. He turned and grabbed Madeleine's wrists. Hug-a-Bug fell from her grasp onto the stone. She was completely off balance and Freddie couldn't hold her. She slipped over the edge, screaming and crying, just her hands still visible as she scrabbled at the stone and sand for any kind of grip.

They ran one at a time across the bridge. Time seemed to slow down and then stop, turning from gas to liquid to solid. Freddie was down on his chest, holding onto Madeleine's fingers, but it couldn't possibly be enough. She was nearly gone.

'Help me!' he shouted.

Gwen dived forwards. She reached over Freddie and gripped a wrist, then the other, painfully tearing one of her nails.

Imagine the old me with a torn nail, she thought, sweat breaking out across her face. I would have been

115

traumatised for days. What a pathetic person I was. Now...

'Now you're amazing,' grunted Freddie, picking up her thoughts. 'But don't stop pulling, though.'

Madeleine was still screaming and Gwen was hanging on with everything she had, and Jess was there beside her, doing what she could, not wasting any energy on noise, her breathing steady, her eyes focused.

You are seriously cool, thought Gwen. I wish I was like you.

The mist thickened around them like a damp cloth. Everything was greasy, difficult to grab. Madeleine slipped again. How much longer could they hold on?

Maybe we have to let go, Gwen thought. We did our best. She was never going to make it anyway.

Her fingers cramped and failed her. Gwen had to let go, but Freddie was clearly in no mood to give up. He grabbed and grabbed again. Carter took over, heaving with everything he had. Now it was him, and Freddie, and Jess, playing a deadly game of tug o' war. Slowly, like a snail drifting across a window, Madeleine edged upwards and Gwen looked into her wide, staring eyes.

'I don't want to fall, Gwen,' she cried.

'You won't,' Gwen replied, but it they all knew that was an empty promise. Madeleine didn't have the strength to help herself and that meant they were stuck in a horrible sickening limbo. She would hang there until they were all too tired to hold her any longer.

Gwen screamed, all of her anguish and frustration released in one long echoing howl. At times, this crazy new existence had almost felt like a game. And now, it was nothing at all like that. Now, it all seemed like life and death. There was just the steady beat of Gwen's heart and Madeleine's eyes fixed on her, boring into her soul, pleading to be saved. Long seconds passed. Their hands were slipping, their grip weakening. It would be over very soon.

Gwen felt a rush of warm air. Someone was running across the bridge. He was shouting as he ran. Then the newcomer was heaving Madeleine's shoulders up over the edge.

17

'Let me help!'

George heaved on the shoulders of the girl who was hanging over the edge of whatever it was, wherever the hell they were. He had landed heavily on stone and sand, his head buzzing with the noise of a raven, feathers floating all around him, all the colours of the universe jumbled up in a confusing mess.

As he pulled, he tried to remember anything but his brain wasn't playing the game. It was all a blank fuzzy nothing. Then his head was suddenly full of a horrible painful buzzing noise like dozens of electric drills all revving up at the same time as bits of memories arrived. He was at school. He was in his room. The window...the raven...the tall man...

Slowly, agonisingly, the girl slid up over the lip of the rock column. Her mouth was open and her eyes were wide with terror.

She's got Down's syndrome, he thought, his mind suddenly clear, all trace of dizziness and confusion gone.

What is she doing here? What are any of us doing here?

Four of them - two girls about his age, a boy who glared at him with eyes like blades, and the younger one next to him, pulling as hard as he was.

'I think I know who you are,' the boy said through gritted teeth.

'Do you? Maybe in a minute you can tell me how that's possible.'

'Deal.'

The girl's hands slipped but he doubled his effort and then, just like that, the girl flopped next to him like a landed fish. George collapsed across her, gulping in air, muscles screaming, joints on fire. He looked around for the first time, open mouthed, all the pain and fatigue suddenly forgotten. He was in some insane monstrous mist filled cavern. A huge weapon of some sort glowed overhead, hanging in mid-air. Hundreds of ravens were surging out of the darkness, through the mist, screaming as they flew. And from a tiny crack in the rock two figures emerged – a boy whose hands seemed to drip liquid gold, and the tall man called Ambrose.

'Excellent,' the man said. 'I knew you would do it.'

The boy lifted his dripping hands, and George saw that he was holding a small sword.

'Hi, George. This belongs to you,' he said.

***

Luca wasn't surprised by the look on George's face. He would have looked the same if the roles were reversed.

Ambrose had appeared by the waterfall, and after the shock of seeing him there, with Bran nestled up against him, Luca had listened to all he had to say, delivered in the clipped formal voice that was so different from when he had been Peake. George would need to understand about his dad and who he was, who they all were. More importantly, Luca and the others had to accept that the crossing was an unavoidable task, the only way that the swords would waken and be ready again. The liquid gold was like blood for the blades, but the real magic was the courage and teamwork they had showed in getting across.

Then Ambrose had led Luca back to the chasm, and he had seen the pain on their exhausted faces, and how scared Madeleine looked, but also he could see that they were triumphant. They had done it together.

Luca smiled at Jess, hoping to reassure her. It seemed to work. Reassuring Carter took a bit longer. As always, he was ready to fight anybody who caused him grief, but he calmed down after a while. He was too tired to do much more than throw a few swear words at Ambrose, who took the insults graciously.

There was one more journey across – his mum and McKenna were carried over by Bran and the other ravens, because they had no task to complete, and they wouldn't have made it any other way. So when they were all together, Ambrose waved his arms left and right, and incredible things started to happen.

The cavern was suddenly draped in thick cloth from ceiling to floor, creating a tent. Another wave of his arms brought more drapes down to divide it up into rooms lit by strange green fires that gave off heat but no sparks or smoke, and then a table covered in food and drink. Luca's mouth filled with saliva. His nostrils twitched at the incredible aroma of roast chicken and smoked bacon, pizza, warm bread, cakes and chocolate sauce. Bowls of fruit came next, and even wine for the adults.

The drapes billowed apart and they could see that each of the divided spaces was now a bedroom, kitted out with comfortable looking camp beds, lamps and racks of fresh clothes.

'I've given you the best chance of success,' Ambrose said. 'Rest here. Then find the Great Hall. I think the table will wake the swords once they've been dipped in the gold. I can only hope, anyway. Then use the tunnel. It will always take a sword bearer to where they are most needed, and that will be the girl I mentioned. Her name is Freya. She is waiting for you.'

Luca reached out to touch Ambrose's hand. Their fingers met for the briefest moment and Luca recoiled from the coldness of the touch.

'I'm fading again,' Ambrose said. 'This place, it's too much. Camelot sucks the life out of me. I must go.'

Before he disappeared completely the old wizard smiled and bowed.

'Remember that when you are faced with danger, you have love, friendship and belief,' he whispered. 'Nothing else really matters.'

Then he was gone, and they were left in stunned silence among the splendour of their new surroundings.

'It's a *yes* from me,' said Carter, grabbing some pizza and a chocolate bar. 'That bloke's got talent.'

'Wow.' George was pale and trembling. His eyes didn't leave Luca's. 'I...I don't have any choice but to believe you. To believe all of this.'

'No, you don't.'

'Then I'm grateful that you told me about my dad. I don't know how I feel about it all, but at least he died a hero.'

'Yeah. And I would feel angry if it was me, but he had to keep you hidden. Madoc would have probably killed you if he knew you existed. He does that kind of thing.'

George breathed deeply and rubbed his head, clearly working his way through the madness of it all.

I bet your brain's on fire, Luca thought. Your mum died giving birth to you and you've spent your whole life thinking your dad died in a car crash. You've just found out that he didn't, that he was actually some kind of secret agent and here you are at Camelot holding a sword that means you're the last living descendant of one of King Arthur's knights. Yep. That's a busy kind of day.

'Let's eat,' Luca said. 'We can talk the whole thing through as many times as you want but first, I really need to fill my belly.'

18

'Stop crunching the gears, will you?'

'Sorry, Shorty.'

'Do it one more time and I'm driving.'

'You can't drive,' replied Tallboy.

'Neither can you, by the look of it. Next left in about five miles. And don't miss the turning this time.'

They drove on without speaking. Shorty played with the radio dial but it was mainly static and snatches of pop music. He hated all that stuff – the thudding beats, the stupid voices, the words he couldn't even make out. He wanted something classical. A bit of piano, or some violins. Another twist of the dial filled his ears with a burst of rap. He swore loudly and turned the radio off.

'No wonder kids are all so stupid if that's what they listen to all day,' he grumbled.

'I like that one,' Tallboy replied.

'That doesn't surprise me. There. Turn left. Now, you idiot.'

It was barely a track leading from the road and Tallboy did nearly miss it. There were no streetlights and the rain was falling in a steady curtain that made visibility even more difficult, but that didn't stop Shorty blaming his colleague for every mistake. It was the way things worked between them. Always had been. Always would be. The rules had been agreed in prison a lot of years before and to stay alive, they stuck to the rules.

Shorty was the brains. Tallboy was the muscle. Between them they got the job done and this one was no different, except Shorty had a bad feeling about it, like a seed in your back teeth that you can't quite get out, or the smallest stone in your shoe when you've got to keep on running. He didn't know what it was and that bothered him even more, because he liked to be in control. No – he needed to be in control. Once the control was lost, others had the upper hand, and that made him nervous.

'Tell me again how much money the copper promised us,' Tallboy said.

'Enough to keep you in picture books and sweets for the rest of your life.'

Tallboy laughed and the car sped up and swerved, because he wasn't good at doing two things at once either. Laughing had taken his very slow mind off his driving.

'Careful, you idiot,' hissed Shorty, 'or we'll end up in a ditch.'

Tallboy didn't answer. He fixed his eyes on the road. Shorty glanced at him. The scarred face was half in shadow but he could still see the hurt in Tallboy's eyes.

'Oh, quit the baby sulk, you big lump. I didn't mean anything.'

Tallboy grinned like a happy puppy. He was that easy to control. Shorty, not for the first time, thanked his lucky stars about that. Over the years, Tallboy had got him out of a few narrow scrapes with a quick swing of his fists. He didn't think there would be any need for fighting this time, though. The job was so easy it hardly seemed possible. Find an old woman and take her to the Commissioner. And they had found her, or at least what had happened to her. And after feeding back the information, a change of plan. Move on to the granddaughter. Get her instead.

But there it was again, that niggly feeling. Could it really be that easy? Maybe it would be. Maybe this time they had really landed the jackpot. The plague was a bonus. Lots of the gangs and small-time criminals were out of action, so the rumours went. There was an opportunity for a new player with the cash to build an empire. Shorty had already decided that player was going to be him.

The car bumped along the rutted track. A fox scampered in front of them but he was moving too quickly for Tallboy to react. The car's lights flickered over his muddy fur and reflected in his eyes before he disappeared into a low bank.

'Run, foxy,' Shorty said as they bounced past. 'The bad men are in town.'

'Who?'

'Us, dummy.'

'Oh, I get it. Yeah, run, foxy.'

The track veered left and then right. They were driving out into the wilds now, with no cover. The wind had picked up. The car shifted against it. The temperature was dropping quickly and the rain had worsened. Up ahead, just visible against the grey sky, Shorty saw a windmill with a smudge of light near the top. He guessed they were maybe a mile away.

'Kill the lights,' he growled.

Tallboy flicked them off and they inched forwards in darkness. Now they were both in alert mode, all senses firing. The car nearly left the track a few times but Tallboy had done this kind of thing before and he was earning his money now, taking them nearer and nearer to their target.

'Be alert. It might be a trap for all we know.'

'Just a girl, you said. All alone.'

'I know what I said. Plan for the worst, though. Could be a bloody army in there waiting for us.'

Tallboy's face screwed up in extra concentration as they carried on. Now he was very much ready for a fight that Shorty hoped wasn't coming. Just a girl. He had checked and double checked his sources and the information they had passed him. It all seemed to be genuine. The old lady was dead, and so was her son – rough tough soldier boy, shot down just the other week in the middle of the plague mayhem. And the girl's mum? Hacking into the NHS systems was so easy a five year old could do it. She was gone as well. Plague. So that just left the girl. Thirteen, alone in a windmill miles from anywhere. Shorty licked his lips. Fifty thousand for this. Thank you, thank you, thank you.

'Pull up here. We'll walk the rest of the way.'

Less than a minute later, pistols ready, they slid off through the icy mud, heads down against the wind, bearing down on their target.

19

'So,' mumbled George through a mouthful of scrambled egg and sausage, 'if I've understood it all, Madoc is going to try and release the Black Prince from something called a witch's jar that's held his soul captive for more than six hundred years. Then he's going to drink some of his blood because the Plantagenets were cursed by the devil and he hopes he'll become king of Britain because that's what it says in a spell book written by Merlin the wizard, who's now called Ambrose, and who brought me here to Camelot because I'm the last living descendant of one of King Arthur's knights.'

He paused, chewed a bit more, swallowed, then looked around.

'How am I doing?'

'Ten out of ten,' grinned Carter.

'I know about the Black Prince,' George continued. 'He's buried in Canterbury cathedral. That's where I live. We went there on a school trip a couple of years ago. It's a big marble tomb behind some railings, with a carving of him on the top. Maybe that's where Madoc will go if he gets the girl Ambrose talked about.'

'Oh, yeah,' said Carter. 'I forgot that bit. 'We've got to stop him by finding a girl before he does. And we don't know who she is or where she is. Doddle.'

'Doesn't sound like a doddle. Sounds impossible.'

'We've done the impossible before,' Luca said. 'And I reckon the tunnel in the Great Hall will take us to her.'

'How can you know that?'

'He doesn't,' Carter interrupted. 'If you hadn't already noticed, we kinda make this stuff up as we go along.'

'That's not exactly reassuring.'

'Get used to it.'

'So, I really am in a magical tent next to a bottomless chasm where a few hours ago, or it might have been five minutes, or a year for all I know, I was brought here by a man who is actually Merlin so I could help you lot save Madeleine.'

He picked up a piece of toast from the newly covered tables and waved it in Madeleine's direction. She waved back. Lots of chewing. Lots of agreement. The tent moved gently around them and the smell of the food was almost unbearably good.

'And my dad was really a double agent who hid me from Madoc.' George lifted up the sword from around his neck and held it up to the light. 'And this sword was his. He wore it every day. He knew it would be mine when he died.'

'Top of the class, again,' said Carter.

George looked at Luca.

'You kept it safe for me.'

'Yeah.'

'Thank you.'

George paused, deep in thought, processing everything from the moment a raven had pecked at his window. The others kept munching and waiting.

'How long did it take for you to get your heads around all this?'

'Not sure we really have,' Luca replied. 'Day at a time. I just expect it to keep getting weirder and I haven't been disappointed yet.'

'Good answer,' George glanced at the younger boy, Freddie. 'I don't understand what happened to you at the Tower. That thing with the Black Prince.'

'Why should you?' Freddie snapped. He averted his eyes and began concentrating on a large plate of bacon. 'You weren't there. You have no idea what it was like. You can't see the future or read minds or save the ravens. And you never knew your dad.'

Freddie stopped. He breathed hard, then grabbed a handful of the bacon and stomped off to a dark corner, his back to them all.

'What did I say?' George asked.

'He's just a bit different,' replied Jess. She moved after her brother and they were soon engaged in animated conversation, which was clearly not far off an argument even though they kept their voices low. Luca motioned to George.

'Since that thing at the Tower,' he whispered, 'something's changed. He's just angry like that a lot of the time. Give him a break, yeah? Can't be easy, having a brain wired like that. Hearing what other people think as well as whatever your own brain is screaming.'

'I think he might be on the, you know, on the spectrum?'

'Like autistic?' Carter interrupted.

'Yeah.'

'Man, everybody at my school was like that. On the spectrum this, syndrome that. OCD. ADHD. NYPD.' He paused. 'That last one is a joke.'

'It's not funny,' George said. 'It means he sees and hears things completely differently.'

'No offence, mate,' Carter continued, 'but you've been here five minutes. I think we know a bit more about this than you.'

George held up his hands in agreement.

'Point taken. Just commenting on how I see it. Anyway, I don't want a fight. I just want to get on with it. Eat, move on, find this Great Hall you told me about.'

'Good. All friends again.' Luca this time, relief written all over his face. 'Freddie is just Freddie. He just takes a bit of getting used to, but he saved us before when we were here and I trust him. And Madeleine loves him to bits.'

She had joined Freddie and Jess, holding up a now very dirty Hug-a-Bug for them to cuddle. They were both smiling at her.

'She's great. And I can see you've all got a special bond.'

'Yeah,' Carter said. 'Like the X-men. Welcome to the weirdo club. And shut up, now. I'm starving.'

20

Luca checked them all one more time, for luck. There was no need. They were all ready to leave this strange place, where death had been closer than they wanted to imagine. And yet, as he looked back at the towering columns and the sullen mist that hung over everything, Luca was grateful. George was there now. He liked him. George had the eyes and smile of someone who was happy to fight back. He looked like Randall and he had the same calm presence about him. Now he wore the sword to prove he was that man's son, and so something had gone full circle. Their team was bigger and stronger.

It needs to be, Luca thought. This is going to be harder than saving the ravens. Find this girl who may not want to be found. And then stop Madoc using the darkest magic Ambrose had ever come across.

'Let's go.'

He stood to one side to let them pass. Carter grinned and waved one more sausage sandwich at him. Gwen rolled her eyes. Jess smiled but said nothing. And Freddie stared down at the ground, chewing miserably. Not even Madeleine had been able to lift his mood. And Luca felt that familiar prickle at the base of neck that meant Freddie was wandering around in his head, flitting among his thoughts. Luca looked away.

'I want to see this golden waterfall,' George said.

'Just up there.'

Liz and McKenna brought up the rear. The normal order of things was different here. The adults were just visitors, only present because Ambrose had allowed it. So, they kept back from the discussions and arguments, letting them find their own way. The unspoken rule was that you needed a sword to really understand. They headed off down the tunnel and as the last one of them moved from the pale light into the darkness, the tent melted away.

'All that food, gone,' groaned Carter. 'Some of this magic stuff is too cruel.'

Luca led them to the waterfall. There was only a moment's hesitation before they plunged the swords deep into the cascading gold. The blades sucked up the liquid like parched earth in a thunderstorm and when they took them out, the swords felt different, more responsive, as if they were only asleep rather than dead. Luca looked at his mum, and he didn't think he had ever seen her eyes shine with such understanding as they did at that moment of complete separation between those who had a sword and those who did not.

You're incredible, he thought. I hope I can always make you proud of me.

'Who made this place?' Gwen asked, in awe of the impossible golden cascade. She let it pour over her hands and arms. 'Do you think it was Ambrose?'

Nobody answered, because like everything else here, the waterfall was just another mystery that might never be explained. All they needed to know was that swords had been changed by it. They didn't stay long. There was no way of knowing how far they had to go. An hour later, and after many tight turns and climbs, they passed a chalky wall and stood in some kind of long corridor. Another wall blocked the far end, but that one was covered in intricate carvings of the four animals that Peake had become – the Irish wolf, the Welsh dragon, a Scottish eagle and an English bear, all of the animals intertwined, their faces glaring out at them.

'Not the friendliest of welcomes,' McKenna said.

'What is this place?' Luca asked.

McKenna studied the corridor, a soldier at work, checking angles, distances, escape routes and lines of fire. When he was done, he nodded, satisfied.

'Clever,' he said. 'Very clever.'

'What is?'

'Look around you, Luca. All of you do the same. See it through the eyes of someone who wants to defend it. It's sloped up, for starters. Never much fun, fighting uphill. Then see how it narrows? Nice touch, that. Means no more than one or two are up front at a time.'

Luca followed McKenna's hands as they waved around, pointing out the defensive tricks built into the corridor.

'Yeah, get it. What else?'

'That.'

McKenna pointed at the smooth ceiling. Luca noticed hundreds of tiny black holes dotted all over it.

135

'What are those?'

'Think like a soldier, son. You're in here, crouched down, trying to attack up this tunnel, you and your mates all bunched up together with nowhere to go. What would really ruin your day? I bet you a round trip to the moon those holes can spray you with something unpleasant. Maybe poison gas, or steam, or acid. The human imagination can come up with a lot of ways to hurt. Now, turn around. What do you see?'

Silence. They all stared back down the corridor at the blank wall.

'Nothing,' Freddie said at last, and then he chuckled. A smile broke out across his face, which was a pleasant change from the sullen look that had been there for the last few hours.

'I thought you might work it out, young man,' replied McKenna. 'Go on. Help the rest out here.'

Freddie broke away from the group and stood against the wall. He pretended to fire a gun, then he shot an imaginary arrow, and then he collapsed as if he had been shot.

'Bingo,' McKenna said. 'You're an easy target against that wall. A perfect silhouette. Bang bang you're dead. Although you never hear the bullet that hits you.'

'Or arrow,' added Freddie. 'I think this is somewhere the Black Prince would have enjoyed.'

The smile was gone from his face. He looked older and younger at the same time, and somehow far away.

'You okay, mate?' Luca asked.

136

Freddie blinked and nodded but it seemed to Luca that it took a few more seconds before the boy was completely back with them.

'I'm okay. I sometimes feel like the Black Prince is too close. I don't like that feeling.'

Jess hugged him and the conversation dried up. They stood awkwardly, not sure what to say.

'Important place, then,' McKenna said, breaking the silence. 'Go carefully. There might be all sorts of traps up ahead.'

They eased slowly up the tunnel, lifting up a thin layer of fine sand that looked as if it had been undisturbed for a thousand years. The walls were smooth and curved. Nobody touched them, just in case a careless hand triggered something catastrophic, but nothing happened, and they reached the end of the corridor. Up close, they could see that as well as the carved animals, there were subtle indentations with a zodiac symbol etched into each one.

'Like the Round Table,' Luca said. 'I reckon we should press on the one for our sign.'

He reached out and placed his palm against the Pisces symbol. The others followed his example. As soon as they touched the wall, the rock moved inwards by a few centimetres. It was completely impossible and perfectly understandable all at the same time. This was Camelot, after all. There was magic in every brick and stone. Why shouldn't a massive lump of luck move at the slightest touch?

'Us and doors, eh?' Carter said. 'Always one more to try and get through.'

The rock continued to shift inwards on some invisible mechanism. They didn't even need to push. Their hands were barely touching it.

'Incredible,' McKenna said. 'How the hell are you doing that?'

He touched the rock and it instantly stopped moving.

'Only us,' Freddie said. 'You're not special.'

'If you say so,' McKenna replied, backing away. 'All yours.'

The rock began to move again, faster this time, but leaving no scars as it went. They walked with it. After the rock had travelled about ten metres, it slowed and stopped. They paused, unsure what might happen next. Then the rock began to pivot up from the bottom, like the lid of a tin can folding inwards. Within a minute it was flat against the ceiling. They stepped forwards, hesitant and unsure, bunched up close for safety. They were underneath the stone circle. If it fell, they would be smashed into dust.

And then it did fall, so fast they had no time to even breathe, but instead of crushing them flat the huge stone circle engulfed them and then reformed under their feet. They gasped as one, and grabbed each other in fear and amazement.

They weren't in the corridor any more. They were standing on the Round Table, back in King Arthur's Great Hall.

21

They moved slowly, faces up, mouths open, turning like boats on a lake, taking it all in, except for Gwen. She alone stood still, holding her breath, arms crossed, fists clenched.

'I think it's okay,' she whispered. 'That is, I feel okay.'

'Go, girl,' Carter said. 'I knew you'd be all right this time.'

'You didn't know any such thing, but thank you anyway.'

'That was seriously weird,' Luca said, unable to contain his excitement at what had happened. A moment ago, he had closed his eyes and prepared to die. Now, they had made it to the one place that could take them where they needed to go because behind the banner hanging over the huge fireplace, there was the tunnel. It had helped them before and Ambrose had said it would help them again. Maybe, just maybe, they were getting the hang of it all. They had the swords, they had been dipped in the gold and now the table could make them come alive. The heavy door was still there, of course, but it was undamaged, as if it had been healed of the bullet scars from Madoc's men as they forced their way in. It felt different from the last time. It felt safe.

They showed George what to do with his sword, placing theirs on the zodiac signs carved into the table.

He copied them. The swords glowed and hummed, and it was obvious the magic was back in them. They took the time to explore the hall, because there had been no chance before when the only thing on their minds was survival and escape. Freddie kept his distance from the rest of them, perhaps because his own memory of the hall was different from theirs.

'I'm worried about him,' Luca said to Jess.

She didn't reply, but he wasn't going to give up that easily.

'You two know something and you're not telling us. I can feel it. You've got to tell me, Jess. You can't keep secrets.'

Jess looked away.

'Tell me. You have to.'

'It's complicated,' she said, which was no kind of answer at all and he told her so.

'You're right, but what can I do? He's my brother. I'm just as worried as you are. He won't talk to me and his mind is closed off. I can't read him. I can't see anything. I can't feel anything.'

'You mean...'

'Yes. I can't communicate with him like before.'

'Since when?'

'Since I banged my head in the Shard and he was taken over by the Black Prince. The connection between us is broken.'

'And you didn't think we should know?'

'I'm sorry. It didn't seem that important, and we were back at your flat, and everybody was happy, then your mum got sick again, and then everything since. There just hasn't been a chance to tell you.'

'This is really important, Jess! You and Freddie have been able to communicate like that forever. This has to be something to do with the Black Prince.'

'I know,' she said, and she looked so miserable he wanted to hold her close and tell her he could fix this, but the right words and actions never seemed to come naturally when he most needed them.

'We've got to tell the others.'

'No, please. They already think he's odd. This could make them even more suspicious of him. Promise me, Luca. Promise you won't say anything.'

'On condition you keep a close eye on him. And if you feel anything or sense anything or see anything we need to know about, you have to say.'

'I will but it's like that part of my brain has never really recovered from when I banged it at the Shard.'

'I still think the others should know.'

Just as he finished speaking, Madeleine ran up to them, her face one huge grin. His mum and McKenna were right behind, looking more than a little bit dazed by it all.

'This is really King Arthur's hall?' McKenna asked. 'I mean, *the* King Arthur?'

'Yep,' Luca laughed. 'Crazy, isn't it?'

'Well, let's just say there was nothing in my Army training about what to do if you found yourself in the middle of Camelot, so crazy will have to cover it. Now, where's this magic tunnel I've heard so much about.'

Luca pointed at the banner over the fireplace, then he turned to face Carter, shouting from the other end of the hall. A shimmering white light had appeared high up above them and was now drifting down. It formed into the ghostly knight. He bowed deeply and hovered before them.

'Greetings again, my friends. You made it. How wonderful. And I can see the swords are awake once more. How even more wonderful. I am so very pleased and excited for you. Truly you are deserved of the name knights of the Round Table.'

The ghost drifted lower, but his feet didn't touch the floor. He remained little more than a misty glowing cloud, sometimes more solid, then fading away.

The hall was silent, like a graveyard at midnight.

'How did you get in here?' Carter demanded.

'I don't mean to scare you,' the knight continued. 'I just wished to see you all again, and I was floating this way, and I heard your voices. I can, of course, go anywhere in the castle. And it would appear so can you.'

His dead eyes gleamed as he looked at each of the swords hanging around their necks. Finally, he looked at George.

'A newcomer.'

George looked left and right. All eyes were on him. Luca wondered how the boy would react to this. He didn't have long to find out. George raised himself up and folded his arms. He stuck out his chin.

'George Randall, descendant of the knight Sir Bedivere.'

'Also wonderful. Bedivere was a good friend.'

The knight kept smiling and humming softly. Nobody moved. Luca noticed for the first time that the knight's eyes glinted with more than friendship and humour. He saw something approaching madness, and he felt a surge of fear.

'Nice to see you again,' he said, trying to sound casual and friendly. 'We were, um, just chilling out a bit before we go off and look around a bit more. I'm sure you've got much better things to do than hang around with us.'

'No,' the knight replied, his smile still fixed, his eyes shining brighter. 'I don't. In fact, I think I will stay with you. We can all be friends right here. It will be like old times. All the knights gathered, laughing and sharing stories. And then we can talk about how you're going to help me leave here, at last.'

'Leave here? I don't know what you mean.'

'Well, Pendragon, if you don't know such a thing, that is a shame, but never mind. I can bear the thought of another thousand years now that I have company. No more making do with rats for friends. I have you now, forever!'

He laughed, and the noise was high pitched and unpleasant.

Stay calm, Luca thought. He's a ghost. He can't hurt us. He stretched casually, even faking a yawn.

'What is it?' asked the knight. 'Boring you, am I? Not good enough for the new Pendragon?'

And Luca knew he was right to be a little bit scared, because there was a different edge to the knight's voice.

'Of course not,' Luca said, picking his words carefully. 'Maybe we *could* help you look for a way out. You go one way, we'll go another and meet back here later?'

He smiled his best smile. The knight's eyes narrowed, unsure. Carter started whistling softly.

He's switched on, Luca thought. He knows this could be bad.

'Sounds great, Luca,' Carter said. 'Yeah, let's find a way out.'

Jess was next up, then Gwen. They had all heard the insane laugh. Suddenly, they were a team, moving into position, ready for anything. The knight looked confused and more than a little anxious.

'Stand still. I can't watch you all if you keep flitting around like mayflies. You've been here before. You found the way out on that occasion. Show me.'

'Maybe,' Gwen said.

The knight tensed, if a shimmering ghostly cloud is capable of such a thing.

'You're lying to me. You have no intention of showing me the way out of this prison.'

His voice had risen, the words delivered quickly. The ghost rose up and down in agitation. He headed for Madeleine.

'You, the young one with the strange eyes and the bizarre soft bug thing. You will help me? You will show me the way out of here?'

'Sorry, I can't,' she said.

'Can't or won't? Well, even if the rest of them abandon me, you shall stay.'

'No way,' Freddie shouted, lunging forwards, but Luca had already done the same and they bumped against each other. Luca tumbled, off balance. He held out his hands to break his fall and they passed straight through the ghost. He recoiled from the intense cold. He stood shivering and cradling his arm. The pain was intense, like a freezing toxic injection. The knight smiled sadly.

'You shouldn't have done that, Pendragon,' he whispered. 'You've just felt the touch of the dead. The dark magic will spread through you. That is how I came to be like this and now you will be like me, in this place, for all eternity.'

22

The cold was indeed spreading. It was in Luca's elbow. Now in his shoulder. This was very bad. Luca wanted to squeeze his arms around his body but if he did, they might crack and break off, such was the terrible cold that was gripping him. His heart was racing. The shivering was almost unbearable. Every muscle was firing off, trying to release heat, but it was no good.

'Got to get him out of here,' Carter shouted.

'There is no point,' said the knight, still smiling. 'The cold's got him. Soon, he'll die.'

Luca slumped onto the floor. Even the stones felt warm compared with what was ripping through him. Icy tentacles were spreading along his limbs, heading to his heart and brain. An overwhelming urge to sleep overtook him. He closed his eyes.

'No!'

A painful jab into his arm woke him. Jess was there, gripping his skin, shaking him.

'I can't stay awake,' he said, teeth chattering like bones in a bag.

'You can.'

And then, in his head...

You can and you will. I won't let you die here. Stay with me, Luca. Stay with me!

'I can...hear you...feel you...you can do it, Jess. You can...still...do it...'

Jess was keeping him warm somehow, and it allowed him to stand, but she was suffering as he was improving. Her lips had taken on a horrible blue tinge and her teeth began to chatter.

'Get out of my head,' Luca gasped. 'It's going to kill you as well.'

He stamped his feet down and spread his legs wide for balance, but he was so dizzy he didn't know whether he might fall straight over. Now the others were holding him up and he could feel their warmth. He gripped them hard, panicking, desperate for the cold to fade, wishing beyond anything for the shivering and pain to stop.

'Give him up!' said the knight. 'It's useless.'

'Shut up,' snarled Carter.

Luca's mum pushed the others away and wrapped her arms tightly around him.

'Stay with us,' she said. 'I love you, we all love you. Stay with us!'

'What can we do?' asked George.

'You can't do anything, you fools,' the knight said. 'For the last time, he's going to die.'

He's right, Luca realised.

This was supposed to be a good place, somewhere they could get to know each other, but now it looked like it might be the last place he ever saw. He wanted to get out of the hall. He wanted to be somewhere quiet, dark, warm...

'The tunnel!'

Jess's voice cut through the noise. She was cloudy and indistinct, as if Luca's eyeballs were turning to ice. Every movement hurt. The cold was wrapping itself around his chest, squeezing him, making it hard to breathe. She was no longer in his head.

'Is the cold still in your head?'

'No,' she said.

'That's good.'

He didn't have the energy to say any more. It was nearly over and he knew it.

'Get him up in the tunnel,' Jess shouted again, and after a pause that felt like a million years of agony, Luca was lifted up off the floor. He winced as his frozen muscles shifted to take the strain, but the closeness of the others was helping him stay alive. The knight was screaming in rage. He whipped around in front of them.

'Don't think you can save him. You can't.'

Carter released his grip on Luca and raised his sword. The sight of it caused the knight to fall back.

'You threaten me, son of Lancelot?'

'Too right I do. Get out of the way.'

'Be careful, boy. Touch me and you'll share the same fate.'

'Which tells me you can't touch us first. So you're all mouth and no trousers. Now shift or I'll stick this straight through you and by the look on your pasty face it won't be pretty.'

'Do you believe that puny sword can hurt me?'

Suddenly the knight was staring at six swords, all pointed directly at his head.

'I do.'

The knight drifted away, hovering just out of reach, his face contorted with fury. Gwen's face was close to Luca's. She brushed his cheek and her touch was like fire.

'Last time you saved me. Time to repay the favour,' she said, holding his hand. He grabbed back with all the strength he had left.

'Don't let go of me,' he croaked.

'We won't, mate,' Carter interrupted. 'Can't have you going off on the next adventure without us, eh?'

The hall was now just a whirling blur of blue and grey, and the only sounds Luca could hear were the crunching of his muscles as they fought the cold. In a few moments he would be a ghost, trapped here forever. Somewhere, there had to be some warmth that could save him. Was it at the end of the tunnel? He didn't know, and somehow didn't care, because the cold was pain and pain was the cold, and anything was better than the icicles scratching at the outer reaches of his brain.

'Too...cold...' he said. 'Too...just...too...cold...'

They shoved him up the wall and his elbows scraped painfully against the old brickwork. He didn't know who had already gone up into the space above the fireplace. Somebody had to be there to be pulling him up. Maybe it was Carter. He could certainly hear his voice, shouting and cursing. Then George was shouting and pushing. That was good. They were a real team now, not just a bunch of kids.

'Gonna shove you down, mate,' Carter said. 'Then we'll all follow. Just like when we went to the Shard, yeah?'

Luca nodded in between chattering and shivering. He couldn't speak. He couldn't even see. The ice was in his brain. He could feel it cracking open his thoughts. It was too late...

'Go!'

But before Carter could push, Luca heard his mum scream, and he heard McKenna yelling with pain.

'He flew straight through me!'

'And me!'

Carter hesitated. Luca tried to grab his friend but he had no strength left. His mum was still screaming. The ghost was laughing.

'I'll see what's happened.'

He heard Carter scramble away, curse softly, then he was back next to him.

'Oh, bloody hell,' he gasped. 'He's gone for your mum and McKenna. What a coward, attacking the only ones without swords.'

'Don't...let...them...die...'

He couldn't speak any more. His mouth was frozen solid.

'Sorry, mate. You're out of here.'

Carter shoved him into the tunnel and he was falling, but something was wrong. Just before Carter had pushed, Luca had heard another voice trying to reach him – a voice he recognised from the last time he had been there.

'Arthur...'

He could only manage one word, the effort of speaking unbearable.

There was no reply. The tunnel didn't feel right. It was bucking and shifting, as if some unseen force was pushing it around, changing it, altering it. Luca saw a brief flare of light and then he was falling into nothing. The last time he had done this, it had been over in a flash. This time, the fall seemed to go on and on. He spun and whirled. Flurries of snow lashed him, then jets of flame. Then gentler warmth and a sense of absolute nothing.

How could he fall so far and for so long? Luca relaxed as the cold faded. His muscles eased. The tunnel walls passed by in a steady hum. He slipped into strange dreams, but they didn't last long. He was suddenly bouncing off rocks that should be killing him but instead he was thrown around as if he was in a trampoline park, and it felt so good he actually laughed out loud.

Seconds stretched into minutes. The rocks disappeared. He was still falling through nothing. He could fall like this forever, and that would be the perfect way to spend eternity. Just float away and then go to nothing. What a pleasant thought that was, except there was a new itch at the base of his skull that he couldn't quite reach. The itch grew and grew. It burned like a dozen wasp stings.

'Leave me alone,' Luca groaned.

No chance. The burning was in his brain and he hoped it was Jess trying to reach him, but it could just as easily be his mum losing her battle with the cold, and then he was spinning horribly. At the last moment he braced himself for landing because Luca sensed the ground coming up like a speeding train.

The dust settled. He picked himself up. Nothing seemed to be broken. The cold was gone, but the pain at the back of his head was real enough, and someone was leaning over him – a girl, with wild eyes and dirty skin, and she was pressing a pistol into his neck.

'You've got exactly one minute to convince me why I shouldn't pull the trigger,' she said.

23

'Who...where...?'

'That's five seconds you've wasted.'

Luca scrambled to his feet, which wasn't easy considering the pistol and his general disorientation but she let him, and when he was stood in front of her, he glanced around. He was in a circular room that smelled strongly of wood smoke and old cooking fat. There was an old armchair and one window, covered by a tatty curtain. A clock ticked loudly behind him, counting away the seconds until the girl had promised to shoot him.

'My name's Luca,' he said, pleased to be able to say anything at all, and even more pleased his eyes were working again. 'Luca Broom. I don't know where I am or who you are, but I guess you saw me arrive from nowhere and that it was really scary for you, but please believe me, I'm not going to hurt you.'

The girl laughed.

'What's so funny?' Luca asked.

'I know you're not going to hurt me. I'm the one with the gun, remember?'

Luca's head was spinning. He needed some answers, fast. This was not even close to what he had expected. There was no sign of the tunnel. He was alone here with this strange fierce eyed girl. Yes, the cold had gone from inside him, but it looked like he wasn't going to survive much longer anyway.

'We were all supposed to come here, I think,' he continued, aware that what he had just said made no sense to her.

'Yeah, I did think there'd be more than one of you. The others have gone somewhere else, by the look of it.' The girl lowered the pistol. 'The old man said I should trust you. He said you would tell me the truth. So, Luca Broom, are you the Pendragon or not?'

Now Luca's head almost spun off his shoulders with shock.

'You know?'

'I know lots. For example, I know that there's a bunch of you and that you have the swords, and that Ambrose is actually Merlin. I know what you did at the Tower and I know what Madoc wants. He wants me.'

Luca tried to say anything sensible. Nothing happened. He suddenly felt hot and sick, and his legs buckled like wet paper. He managed to get to the armchair. The girl watched him impassively.

'You don't look great. Oh, and I'm not going to shoot you. I'm saving that for the ones Madoc sends here. That, and a few other surprises.'

Luca coughed and retched. The girl tutted and ran some water into an old stained mug. He drank some of it, grimacing at the unpleasant metallic taste, then splashed some onto his face.

'Bad magic, by the look of it. Serious dark stuff. You're lucky to be alive. My name's Freya, by the way. Freya Morgan. You're in a windmill out in the middle of nowhere on Dungeness marsh, about sixty miles from Canterbury. I'll tell you about me, and this place, and why you're here.' Her voice dropped to little more than a whisper. 'And I'll tell you about the devil's blood.'

***

They told each other everything they knew and everything that had happened.

'Well?' Freya asked. 'What do you think?'

The last traces of the terrible cold had left Luca's body but he still huddled up as if he was in a blizzard, such was the awful memory of what he had gone through. He had heard everything Freya had said but all he could really think of was his mum and McKenna, and that unless the others had managed to get them into the tunnel, they were most likely now ghosts.

'It's all crazy, of course,' he said, 'but then everything is completely bonkers these days. And it fits in with what Ambrose told us about what Madoc was planning, and about you.'

'He knows a lot.'

'More than he lets on, I think.'

'Maybe that's the point. He's like a conductor and we're the orchestra, working it out for ourselves.'

'Yeah. So if I've got it right from what you've said, you were always going to be involved in this at some point because your nan was a witch.'

'Yes.'

'She was directly related to another witch called Morgan le Fay, who was King Arthur's half-sister. That makes you a witch as well.'

'Yes. And means you and me are kind of like half cousins, or something.'

'Yeah, I guess so. One of your witchy ancestors cursed the Black Prince and killed him, trapping his soul inside a pot as revenge for him going back on some promise of sharing power once he was king.'

'Yes.'

He paused, barely able to believe the words coming out of his own mouth.

'Go on,' Freya said.

'Your dad couldn't handle it and he left. Your mum brought you here after your nan died because she understood what you were and was scared that you might be targeted. Finding a real witch could be very exciting for lots of bad people. You know how to do magic, especially the dark stuff. Your mum got the plague and then she left, and then Ambrose came here with Bran, and told you all about me and the others. He said we would appear, just like that, because the only thing that matters is stopping Madoc getting hold of you. He wants to take you to the Black Prince's tomb so that you can reverse the spell and release his soul. He thinks the Prince will be real enough for him to get some of his blood. He thinks it will make him king.'

'Crazy lunatic stuff, eh? Just imagine being mad enough to want to drink the blood of some dude who's been dead for six hundred years. What's wrong with a can of Red Bull?'

Freya laughed at her own joke, and her face softened. Behind the dirt and the aggression, Luca sensed she was just another lost kid.

'And so here I am. Just me. I have absolutely no idea where the others have gone or if they got out of Camelot. And my mum is probably dead. Actually, worse than dead.'

'That's an unpleasant spell,' Freya shivered. 'My nan knew how to do it but she never told me. Not good, making ghosts. Not good at all. You were half frozen when you arrived, like a ghost. I reckon that's why something went wrong. You took some of the dark magic into the tunnel and it didn't like it.'

'So, where the hell are the others?'

'Either still there,' she said, 'or wherever else the tunnel decided to send them.'

Luca checked his phone. No bars.

'You won't get a signal out here.'

'Can't you magic me up a connection?'

'You've still got a lot to learn. It really doesn't work like that.'

So what do we do? Where do we go?'

'We don't go anywhere. We wait. Your friends might find a way here. Maybe Madoc won't find me. Maybe he will. If he does, we'll be ready.'

'Too many maybes for my liking. We can't just sit here for days. I need to find my friends, and my mum and McKenna. I need to get back to Camelot.'

'Not happening. Look around you, Luca. The tunnel disappeared the second you fell out of it. There's no way back.'

'Then I'll walk.'

'Lousy idea. We're miles from anywhere. The marsh is lethal. One wrong step and you're up to your neck in freezing mud. And, by the way, I reckon it's about three hundred miles. Unless you can get your raven mates to take you, you're going nowhere.'

Luca knew she was right. He was stuck there. He looked around, thinking. Then he saw the photograph. His heart missed a beat.

'That's you?'

'Yeah. Me and the folks in happier times. Last saw dad up at the Tower. You might have bumped into him there. I hope he's okay.'

'Your dad was there,' Luca said, unsure how he was going to say what had to be said.

'Really? That's fantastic!'

'Freya, there's something you have to know.'

'What is it?' she demanded. 'Tell me.'

'I'm really sorry,' Luca continued, his mouth dry. 'He was killed by Madoc's men.'

Silence, then, except for the clock's tick and the rattle of the window pane as the wind roared outside.

Freya closed her eyes. When she opened them, a single tear ran down her cheek.

'Thanks for being there, Luca. At least I know what happened.'

'There was nothing we could have done. It was an ambush.'

Luca looked down. Twice now, he'd done this. First telling George, and now Freya. It was horrible, and he remembered discovering about his own dad's death, and how somehow they all had something in common. He took out his own memento and held it up for Freya to see. She gazed at the photograph without speaking.

'I carry this all the time.'

'I can understand why.'

Freya suddenly looked away, at the grimy window, then towards the kitchen door.

'I can hear something...'

A hideous crashing noise echoed up to them from the bottom of the windmill, followed by harsh shouting and cursing.

'We're out of time, Luca. They've found me,' Freya said. 'Come on. This way!'

24

She grabbed Luca's arm and pulled him behind the battered old armchair. If this was the best hiding place she had planned, he didn't feel that confident about their chances of escape. Camelot felt like a lifetime ago. As had become so normal, he was suddenly in a completely new but equally dangerous situation. He had no idea what he might up against. He had only met Freya an hour before. If she was right and this was Madoc come to get her, he was in serious trouble.

'The door was supposed to hold them up,' Freya said. 'I should have done better. Maybe the traps will get them.'

The voices had fallen silent. Luca strained to hear anything. Someone was scraping around down there. Then he heard a series of loud metallic clangs, followed by shouting, calling Freya's name, telling her there was nowhere to hide, that she was trapped and not to do anything stupid.

'They've got past the traps,' snarled Freya.

That didn't sound good to Luca.

'Apart from a door that didn't hold them and traps they seem to have skipped over, what else have you got?'

'My pistol.'

'Right.'

The footsteps increased in volume and intensity, slammed down on each stair with such force the wooden floor shook underneath them.

'Don't be stupid, Freya!' a man shouted, clearly not worried about making any noise. 'Come on out. There's a good girl. We won't hurt you.'

'They won't,' Freya whispered. 'They need me alive, remember.'

'They might not be that friendly towards me,' replied Luca.

Then the kitchen door creaked open. A torch beam flicked across the ceiling and walls. Luca froze. They would be found in seconds.

'Your sword,' Freya whispered.

'What?'

'Your sword. Look.'

The blade was glowing.

'Why's it doing that?'

'I don't know.'

'You don't know?'

'Like you said, I've still got a lot to learn.'

The men were in the kitchen, shining the torch around.

'I'm not in the mood for hide and seek,' one of them said. 'Show yourself.'

The sword was humming, coming alive, ready to do whatever it needed to do. Luca closed his eyes. He focused on the blade, concentrated his thoughts onto the tip of the metal. He squeezed the sword's handle, letting his arm become an extension of it, feeling the heat and the energy travel up to his brain and back down again.

Focus...focus...focus...

'Get ready,' he said.

Then he jumped up from behind the sofa and pointed the sword towards the door, with no idea how many of them were there or whether they were armed. He was acting on pure instinct now, trusting the sword to do what he needed it to do.

'There!'

The torch shone directly in Luca's face, dazzling him. He dipped to one side, keeping the sword up. A thin beam of light shot from the blade, rapidly spreading out into a complex spider's web of interconnected gold threads that wrapped themselves around what Luca could now see was two men, one short and wiry, the other huge and muscular with a ferocious scar down his face.

The shorter man was holding the torch and a gun, and Luca ducked as the man fired it wildly. He felt the air above him shift apart as the bullet sped past and the room was filled with noise and acrid smoke. The gold web tightened around the men and the gun fell to the floor, out of the man's reach. He cursed and swore, spitting out his anger as he struggled to get free.

'Now's our chance!' Luca shouted.

He turned back to see if Freya had responded, and sure enough she was next to him, focused and alert, back in control, her own pistol up ready to fire.

'No!'

'Why not? They were going to shoot you.'

'That's not a good enough reason to do the same.'

Freya's arm hovered for a few moments, the silence broken only by the constant swearing and growling from their captives.'

'You'd better be sure about this.'

'I am. We can't just kill them, Freya. Do that and you're no better than them.'

She lowered the pistol.

'Let's get out of here while we can.'

They edged past the two men, who had now stopped struggling.

'Sorry to leave you all tied up like this,' Luca said.

'You'll be more than sorry when we get out of here,' replied the shorter man.

Freya led the way down the stairs, through the traps, most of which had been fired off by a broom.

'I left that there. So stupid.'

'Don't beat yourself up. We've got away. That's the only thing that matters.'

Then she turned and ran back up the stairs. Luca yelled after her but she was back in moments, her photograph held up for him to see.

'Only thing I need from this place.'

The door of the windmill had been smashed down. The wind and rain were driving in, soaking the floor, forming dirty puddles on the uneven flagstones. Freya grabbed a thick oilskin coat that was hanging by the door. She shoved the photo frame into a pocket. Then she took down another coat and handed it to Luca.

'It was my mum's. You'll need it out there.'

She was right. Within seconds, the rain had soaked Luca's hair. He cleared his eyes again and again, but it was no use.

'Which way?'

'Straight down the track. If you go off it you're drowned. We need to get as far away as we can. How long will that web last?'

'Not a clue.'

'Then we've got to put some distance between us and them.'

'Scary looking, weren't they?'

'Scary? More like absolutely terrifying. They really were going to kill you, Luca.'

He didn't answer. Suddenly, horribly, violently, it was game on once again.

25

George's head thudded like a hammered nail. Everything was noise and swirling wind, and images of ghosts and dark tunnels, and blizzards and scorching sun. The knight had been so close he could still smell his breath, stale like a damp cave, and he had tried to help Luca's mum but there was nothing he could have done, and anyway none of it felt real because he was suddenly back at school, on the lawn where Ambrose had stood under his window. The broken glass had been covered with a neat square of plywood, but apart from that one ugly scar, everything else looked exactly as it always had. Neat clipped grass, well maintained buildings, smooth tarmac. Woods was gone and George wondered if he had ever been there.

It was dark, which meant nothing any more. George had no idea what day it was. Somebody touched his face.

'It's me,' said Madeleine. 'Where are we?'

'My school,' George replied. 'Canterbury.'

'That's no good. We were supposed to go to where the girl called Freya lives.'

'Well, we're not there. We're here.'

'I didn't like any of that tunnel thing,' she added. 'I could see lots of things in my head and some of them were scary but it felt like Bran and his friends were there with me. They talked to me all the way. It helped. I don't know where they are now.'

George nodded, in the dark, because he didn't have anything to say in response. The reality of it all was suddenly too much. Madeleine was talking about magic tunnels and ravens like other kids might mention football teams or homework. He took her hands and did his best to reassure her, but it was difficult when he was so shaken by it all. He heard whispers somewhere close by. It was Jess and Freddie, instinctively quiet, keeping low, checking it all out. George peered into the darkness. No sign of anybody else.

'How did we end up here?' he asked.

'Don't know,' said Jess. 'That wasn't like the last time. It was too juddery, like the tunnel didn't really have much control of us.'

'Where are the others?'

Nobody could answer that.

Luca wasn't there, and of course the adults hadn't made it. He blinked away the image of them freezing to death, already transparent as the dark magic ripped through them. One minute they had been a team, swords full of energy, ready to go and rescue the girl, and the next this catastrophe.

The school was deserted. The sight and smell of the place was strangely reassuring, and even though it wasn't somewhere he had ever been truly happy, at least now he had an understanding of why he had been here at all. He thought of his dad, living a life of danger and denial, sacrificing so much, and he wished more than anything that he could be there now to share it all, and that he could tell him he loved him.

He wrapped the others in a tight bear hug for no other reason than he needed to, and it helped. The overwhelming sense of being alone faded.

'You can let go now,' Freddie mumbled.

'Yeah. Sorry.'

'Don't apologise,' said Jess. 'I understand.'

He wanted to say so much more, about this place, about Camelot, and about all of them, but there was no chance because just then Carter appeared out of the shadows, eyes wide, mouth open, panic scored across his face.

'You all right?' George asked. 'We thought nobody else had made it.' He paused. 'Is Gwen with you?'

'No!'

And then the reality of their situation hit home. No Luca. No Gwen. The adults almost definitely dead. They weren't where they were supposed to be. It wasn't looking so good.

26

'Where am I?'

Nobody answered Gwen's question. The shops were open and people shuffled around, and the streets hummed to the sound of traffic, and the lights were on but nothing really felt normal. Her head was full of strange noise. The lights were too bright. The journey through the tunnel had been long and terrifying and it appeared she had travelled alone.

'Where am I?' she repeated, louder this time.

'In my face,' somebody shouted nearby. A boy of maybe fifteen, hoodie up, dirty wet trainers. For a second she thought it was Carter, and she smiled, but the shadows moved and she saw it was nobody she knew, and the boy's face was full of fear and anger.

Gwen backed away. She bumped into somebody else, a woman dragging along a wailing child.

'Watch it,' the woman snarled.

Gwen muttered an apology and moved on, avoiding any more eye contact with the crowds because too many of the eyes were dull with shock and grief, and plenty more shone madly with the relief of unexpected survival. The plague was gone but the consequences of it were everywhere.

She staggered along a few streets, past the shops and pubs that had opened again in the hope there were still customers for them. She didn't notice the drizzly rain or the puddles, her feet so wet she might as well have just been swimming.

What's happened? Where are the others?

The panic was overwhelming, like it was something solid threatening to crush her down to nothing. It took everything she had to control her breathing. Slowly, second by endless second, her heart rate settled. Her vision cleared. The sounds and colours settled back to something approaching normal. She headed off again, retracing her steps, trying to find where the tunnel had dropped her.

She found herself at the top of what a sign told her was St Margaret's Street. She moved on across the High Street and into Mercery Lane. She hurried to the Old Buttermarket, with a narrow opening into Burgate to the right and Sun Street to the left. She could see through the arch of what looked like some kind of gatehouse, and the building that rose above the cramped shops could only be a cathedral, and she immediately knew where she was.

'I'm in Canterbury,' she whispered, and the sound of her voice seemed to bounce off the ancient walls around her, amplifying into a great noise that the whole world could hear, but of course it was only really in her head, and the cathedral's great towers and spires stood as silent as they had done for a thousand years, and the people who pushed past her did not care who she was or why she was there, or how indeed she had got there in the first place.

Something scratched at her neck. She felt for the sword. It was suddenly warm, but not in a pleasant way. More like the heat from a nettle rash, or sunburn, and for the first time since she had first placed it over her head, Gwen didn't like the feel of it there.

The Black Prince is close, she thought. The sword knows it, too.

She didn't know what to do or where to go. If the others had come through to a different part of the city, how could she possibly find them? And if they weren't here at all, if they had gone to where they were supposed to go, to the girl that Ambrose had said was waiting for them…

No. That wasn't a thought she wanted to have. They must be here. Maybe she should just stay where she was. They might be looking for her. They would pass here sooner or later. But that might be hours, or days. And the rain was coming down heavily, and it was cold.

Gwen shivered, remembering that awful alone feeling when she had run from the Shard.

Stay calm, she told herself. Think.

She moved across to the gatehouse, out of the rain. Fewer people were around now that the weather had closed in. It was getting dark more quickly than she liked, but at least it was dry under there. Gwen squatted down, utterly exhausted.

Maybe just sleep for five minutes, she thought, letting her eyes close.

She came to with a jump, lashing out at whoever was shining a torch in her face.

'Steady, girl. Steady.'

Gwen squinted into the light.

'Leave me alone.'

'Of course, if you want me to, just as soon as I know you're not harmed or in danger.'

The torch light dropped across her, and Gwen saw it was a woman in her fifties, dressed in sensible outdoor clothes with a woolly beanie pulled down close to her eyes. The woman had a friendly face and kind eyes, and she was looking at Gwen with obvious concern.

'I was passing by and I saw you all curled up, asleep. You shouldn't be out in this filthy weather.'

Gwen couldn't really disagree with that, but she said nothing.

'I'm not interested in who you are or why you're under there. Plenty of kids lost parents recently, eh? I just want to be sure you're okay.'

'Thanks,' Gwen replied. 'I appreciate it.'

They looked at each other for a few moments, as the rain hammered down outside the gatehouse.

'You staying there all night?' the woman asked.

'I don't know. Maybe when the rain stops I'll head off. My friends are somewhere nearby, I think. We got separated when...when the rain began.'

'Not from here, are you?'

'No.'

'I don't like to leave you. Why don't you come with me and we'll get you warm and dry. I've got some hot chocolate and bread just waiting to be toasted. It's around the corner.'

Gwen paused, trying to work out what to do, but there was really no choice. It wouldn't be long before hypothermia set in.

'You're not some kind of murderer, are you? I mean, you hear all sorts of stories.'

The woman laughed.

'That's funny. Do I look like one? The only thing I could murder is a cup of tea and some of that toast. With jam.'

That decided it.

'Okay. Just for a bit, though. And don't think you can ask me loads of questions. I won't tell you anything.'

The woman ran a finger across her lips. Gwen smiled, relief flooding through her. This might be the chance she was hoping for. Something to eat, dry her clothes, maybe even a bed for a few hours. In the morning, she could find the others, if they were in Canterbury.

They walked in silence, side by side. Gwen's eyes darted left and right but there was nobody else around. The woman pointed at a house set back from the road.

'There we are.'

Gwen followed her through the heavy front door, down the tiled hallway and into the kitchen. It was cold inside, as if the heating was an afterthought, and Gwen shivered.

'I'm sorry,' the woman said. 'I try not to heat the place too much. Costs a lot, you know. Let me get you some blankets. Pop the kettle on, will you?'

She bustled past and Gwen heard her go upstairs, singing softly as she went. The kitchen was tidy and more modern than Gwen had expected. There were plenty of mugs in a cupboard and six chairs around the smart oval table. The hot chocolate was unopened, in front of boxes of flavoured herb teas.

The kettle boiled quickly, its glass lit up by a cool blue light. The woman was coming back downstairs. She held out three thick fleece blankets as she drifted into the kitchen.

'These will help warm you up. And don't worry about the drinks. I'll make those.'

Gwen slumped into one of the chairs and pulled the blankets around her shoulders. The woman put a mug of hot chocolate in front of her. Gwen nodded her thanks and sipped the hot drink. The woman sat opposite, hands wrapped around a cup of tea.

'I know you said no questions, but I'm a good listener, and I can't help be worried about you, wandering around in the rain.'

'Thanks, but I don't want to talk about anything. I'm just grateful for your help.'

They both went back to their drinks, eyes down. Gwen had stopped shivering. The warmth was returning to her limbs, and her face was flushing up, lips tingling from the chocolate. Her eyes drooped and she sat upright, fighting off the fatigue.

'You look done in,' the woman said. 'Finish your drink. I've got plenty of room here. Stay the night. Start again in the morning, eh? All fresh and rested.'

Gwen didn't think she had ever heard anything so perfect in all her life. She tried to stand up but her legs were suddenly too wobbly to hold her up. She fell forwards across the table.

'Sorry,' she slurred. 'I'm just so tired.'

'Of course you are, dear,' the woman smiled. 'Time for bed.'

Gwen climbed the stairs on her hands and knees. She pushed open a door and toppled onto a bed. She tried to speak but her lips felt like raw sausages and her eyes no longer wanted to focus on anything. She snuggled under the duvet, vaguely aware of the woman still chatting to her, and her brain made one last attempt to function.

'I...I...'

'You're not going anywhere,' the woman said, and just before she plunged into the deepest, blackest sleep she had ever known, Gwen saw that the woman wasn't smiling any more.

27

It was so cold that Luca's teeth chattered even as he ran. His feet crunched through dirty ice. His red fingertips stung. He couldn't feel his face. Blinking was painful, as if a thin sheen of ice cracked on the surface of his eyeballs each time.

'Which way?'

Freya simply pointed and kept running. Luca stumbled along. His mind replayed what had happened, like a slow-motion movie, each frame splashed in the light of the gun going off, and how close he had come to being shot. The golden web had surged from the sword with a mind of its own, and even though it had allowed them to escape, it unsettled him how little he knew of the sword's power or how to control it.

The windswept road was deserted. Nobody else was crazy enough to be out at three in the morning when it was cold enough to freeze the steam off your skin. Salt spray burned his lips, whipping in from the sea. He hunched lower into the borrowed coat and sped up, pounding the cracked tarmac like a marathon runner in the final stages of a race, desperate to cross the line. There was nothing around but the thick oily darkness and the knowledge that he was separated from his only friends in the whole world.

I never wanted this, he thought. I never wanted any of this.

'Keep up,' Freya muttered.

'Decided yet where we're headed?'

'Somewhere. Anywhere. Just keep up.'

'We need to get a car, or something.'

'Can you drive?'

'No. Can you?'

'Can't be that hard. Point and steer.'

'Yeah,' Luca replied, in no mood to argue. 'Simple as that.'

'We can rest for a minute, if you like,' said Freya, her tone softening a little. 'Just a minute, though. Once your muscles stiffen you've had it.'

Luca squatted down. He closed his eyes and took a few deep breaths. The briny air tasted good. It cleared his head. He tried to picture the others and what they would be doing. It helped to think of them. It made them feel close, somehow.

'Your mates any good at directions?'

'Suppose so. Depends where they are.'

'You hope they're in Canterbury?'

'Of course. Dumb question.'

'That's the last place I want to be, though.'

'Where, then? You've got to decide. We need food, dry clothes, money, something to drink.'

'I'm thinking.'

Luca's muscles had indeed started to stiffen. His thighs burned and his knees ached. This was hopeless.

'Come on, Freya. Think. We need a plan, starting with not freezing to death out here in the middle of nowhere.'

'So let's get on with walking. You're the one sat in the road looking like he might cry.'

That was enough for Luca. He was up on his feet in a second and pacing away. It took a few seconds for him to register that Freya was laughing.

'What's so funny?'

'You are. Boys are so obvious. Make you feel a bit pathetic and you have to show us how big and hard you are. Works every time.'

'I thought you'd spent your whole life in the windmill with no friends?'

The laughing stopped. Freya's eyes were dark shadows. She bit her lip.

'In my head, I've had lots of friends. Only in my head, though.'

'Well,' Luca said, 'Come with me to Canterbury. Find the others. You'll have plenty of real friends.'

'Cheap attempt to get me to say yes.'

'Guilty. What do you say?'

'You promise?'

'Promise.' Luca looked away. Promises were easier to make than keep. 'And they'll help to keep you safe. Between us, we can stop Madoc properly this time.'

They set off again, hugging the coast. It wouldn't get light for hours yet. The darkness would help to hide them. The road was dimly lit but it was dead straight.

Up ahead, Luca saw low buildings and parked cars. A dog barked somewhere and he jumped at the unexpected sound. A light flicked on at a window.

'We're too exposed out here,' Freya said. 'They could have escaped that web thing. Be looking for us. There could be more of them here.'

'Yeah. We need to go faster.'

Freya started to jog. Luca couldn't believe the energy the girl had. His own legs felt like chains dragging over wet concrete.

The light went out. Someone getting up to visit the toilet or woken by a nightmare. There must have been plenty of those recently. More barking, then shouting at the dog, telling it to shut up. A car coughed into life. The stillness of the night was gone. Luca felt the whole world was waking up and that wasn't good. They had to stay anonymous and unseen.

'Off the main road,' Freya called as she swerved into an alley. Luca followed. A right, a left, then another right onto a deserted street parallel to the coast road. The car noise receded, heading the other way. It was quiet again, except for the soft padding of Luca's trainers and the drum beat of his heart.

Fresh energy kicked in to his muscles. He was alert and fully awake, his senses tuned in to any possible danger. They moved like ghosts through the town. After fifteen minutes they were nearly back on the coast road. Luca's confidence grew. Maybe there had been nothing to worry about. Maybe there had. Either way, he was ready to push on. A quick sprint across to the road. Freya nodded and smiled, even raised a hand for a clumsy high-five.

As she did, headlights exploded into life, blinding them.

'Don't move!'

Luca recognised the voice - one of the men from the windmill, calmly threatening.

'Keep those hands up. I don't know what that web trick was or how you did it but I don't want to see it again. Walk slowly towards me. Run away and you're dead.'

Luca's mind was racing. They were trapped, but that didn't stop him looking for any way to escape. There was a low wall nearby, between him and a pebbly beach. Maybe, just maybe, he could dive behind it. Maybe the sword would work again.

'Do as I say. Last time you were lucky. You won't be lucky twice.'

They both stood motionless. Luca glanced at the wall one more time.

'Sonny,' the man said, 'I don't like you. I don't like what you did to me but sadly for you it didn't last very long. Feel free to give me an excuse to shoot you.'

It was over and they both knew it. Luca and Freya raised their hands and walked towards the lights.

28

George led them through the grounds of the school.

I never gave you a chance, he thought, staring at the silent old buildings. I'm sorry. Maybe if I'd known the truth I could have been happy here.

But there wasn't time to dwell on the past. What mattered now was finding Luca and Gwen, then they had to focus on Madoc and what he was planning. It was best to get out of there and melt into the city. And because the tunnel had dumped them here, George felt like he was to blame and that he had to put things right.

'That way,' he said, pointing at the archway where he had first met Ambrose. He had known then that there was something different about the man. He had sensed something was coming.

'Where the hell are you going, Randall?'

Woods was striding towards him.

'Friend of yours?' Carter asked.

'Not exactly.'

'Do you want me to sort him out?'

'No. Leave it.'

Woods was up close all of a sudden, chin out, arms crossed.

'Where have you been, Randall? You've got some explaining to do.'

George paused.

'What do you mean? How long have I been away?' he asked.

'What sort of a question is that, dumb brain? A few days, of course.'

His answer just added to the sense of disorientation that was overwhelming George. Day and night, time and place no longer seemed to mean anything.

'We haven't got time for this idiot,' Carter added.

Woods turned on his heels, eyes narrowed.

'I'm sorry, I don't remember giving you permission to exist.'

That was enough for Carter. One swift punch to the cheek was all it took. Woods was on the ground, sprawled in the mud.

'Can we go now?' he asked.

'Follow me,' said George. 'Thanks for that, I think.'

'Any time.'

Now that Carter had acted, George wanted more than anything to drag Woods to his feet and knock him down again. As he moved in, Jess put a hand on his shoulder and pulled him gently around to face her.

'He's not worth it.'

'Isn't he?'

Jess shook her head.

'You're like Luca. All that anger, always ready to lash out. Let it go, George.' Jess held his gaze. She didn't blink. 'Let it go.'

And George knew that Woods could never hurt him again because his new friends were the only thing that mattered now.

'You're right. Luca and Gwen are out there,' he said. 'We don't stop looking until we find them.'

'Starting now,' shouted Carter. 'Get a move on.'

They ran through the archway and into the narrow cobbled street beyond.

'Which way do you think?' Carter asked.

'Not a clue,' George replied.

Carter turned to Freddie.

'Use your clever brain. Find them.'

'I'm already trying,' Freddie said. 'Gwen's close. I can't sense Luca anywhere.'

'How do you know that, Freddie?' George asked.

The younger boy just tapped his forehead and jogged on down the street.

'Telepathic stuff,' Carter said. 'Just roll with it.'

Freddie led them through a maze of streets until they reached the gatehouse. He paused, head cocked to one side, almost sniffing the air like a hound on a scent.

'She was here. I know it. She was hiding from the rain, wondering where we were. Somebody found her. She spoke to them. She went away with them.'

'Where is she now?' Carter demanded.

Freddie's face was scrunched up with concentration.

'Come on, Freddie. Where is she?'

'She...she...she's...' Freddie's shoulders sagged. His head dropped forwards onto his chest. 'She's gone, Carter. I don't know where she is.'

They stood quietly in the archway, occasionally looking up at the cathedral.

'Feels like a dead end,' Carter said. 'I didn't think this would happen.'

Freddie walked towards the massive building and George noticed that he suddenly seemed different in the way he moved. Then Freddie turned to face them and George shivered, because the boy's eyes were pitch black and when he spoke it was in another voice.

'Close...so close...keep coming closer...your friends are coming too, and my sword is so close...'

Freddie's eyes cleared and he slumped to the ground, groaning and holding his head.

29

Somebody was speaking at Gwen but the words seemed to be coming from a very long way away, and in a foreign language. She couldn't capture a single sensible thought, such as where she was or what had happened. Everything was a useless muddle.

Need to wake up, she told herself. Wake up...

'Wake up!'

A light was flashing in her eyes and the words were real, not just her own thoughts. She turned her head away from the light but a rough hand brought her back under its glare.

'Wake up, Miss Madoc. And stop struggling. There's no point.'

Gwen couldn't see who was speaking but the voice seemed familiar. Her drugged brain searched for the right memory. Where had she heard him before? Where...

She choked as a bottle of water was placed against her lips and the contents were tipped into her mouth. After a few gulps, the bottle was removed.

'Good. You're nearly back with us. I thought she'd given you too many sleeping tablets.'

It was coming back to her – Canterbury, the rain and cold, the friendly woman who had turned out to be anything but, and the hot chocolate that tasted so good but had made her so very sleepy. Now she understood why. She blinked and swallowed, brain now functioning apart from a steady headache. She looked around. She was still in the bedroom so they hadn't moved her whilst she was unconscious. That was good, at least, but suddenly she placed the voice, and she gasped.

'You!'

The man lowered the torch and she pulled away in fear.

'Yes,' Gabriel replied. 'Me. And you know what that means. He's here as well.'

The door opened.

'Hello, my dear,' Madoc said. 'Family reunion time.'

Gwen didn't know if she could speak, and her heart was beating so rapidly it was almost painful. Madoc approached her like a cat stalking a mouse. There were new lines around his eyes and she noticed a slight limp, but he still radiated the same constant power. He smiled, but there was just ice in the smile.

'Anyway, let's talk about the important things in life. Starting with why you were alone when my very efficient agent found you. You forgot I have eyes and ears everywhere. You were too easily fooled, Gwen. A simple promise of a bed for the night and hot chocolate, which tells me you were not in any way prepared for being out in the cold and rain. So where are your friends?'

Gwen said nothing. Madoc shrugged and tried again.

'You don't know or you don't want me to know?'

Still nothing. She stared ahead, mouth clamped shut.

'Well, that's clearly how you want to play this. I can do it your way. I'll just tell you how I see it and watch your response. You can't hide anything from me. You're my daughter.'

'No, I'm not,' she hissed before she could stop herself.

'You always were a fiery girl,' Madoc laughed, and Gwen thought she heard a hint of sadness in his voice. 'Like your mother.'

It took every bit of self-control Gwen could muster not to react. She controlled her breathing, closed her eyes, and waited for him to speak again.

'Very good,' Madoc said. 'I would have been disappointed if you'd bitten so easily. Okay, Gwen. Here goes. You and your charmless friends ran away from the Tower after our last meeting. I suspect you all ended up in Winchester at Broom's house? Yes, I can see I'm right. And then my sudden reappearance spooked you back to Camelot. I know there were odd happenings in Winchester and at the Tower. Lots of ravens, strange weather, the usual theatrics whenever Merlin is around.'

He raised his eyebrows. Gwen did her best to remain entirely passive but he was right. It was impossible not to show some emotion under his unwavering stare. She blinked and looked away.

'Excellent. My suspicions were right. Then I have to fill in the gaps here, but I would imagine Merlin has warned you all what he thinks I'm going to do and told you to stop me. He always likes others to do his dirty work for him. I don't know exactly what he knows but the very fact you're in Canterbury shows me I'm right. I didn't expect you to be alone, and I'll find out why, but for now let's just say everything is working out beautifully.'

Gwen lowered her head. The situation looked desperate. Madoc sighed and sat down next to her on the bed. She shuffled away.

'Gwen,' he said,' his voice quieter, 'it doesn't have to be like this. There's still another way. You know I'm going to win, eventually. I will have what our family have always deserved and you can join me. I'm willing to forgive your mistakes. Tell me where your friends are. Come with me to the cathedral. Help me get what is rightfully mine.'

That was too much. Gwen turned to face her father.

'You want me to betray my friends? You want me to fall in with your insane plan to drink the blood of the Black Prince? You want me to forget everything you've done and go back to playing happy families?' She sneered at him. 'You're mad as well as evil. Find your Devil's blood, then go to hell.'

Madoc said nothing for a long time, their eyes locked. Then he threw back his head and roared with laughter.

'Wonderful! You've just told me everything, Gwen. You do know about the blood and that means you were heading for the cathedral. Thank you so much. You've just made it all so much easier for me.'

He stood up and headed for the door.

'And one last thing. Merlin might have mentioned a girl. You've failed there as well. She's currently on the way here, together with my prize catch of the day. Luca Broom.'

He was still laughing as he left.

30

The car bounced along the quiet side roads, turning at intervals until they were headed on a dual carriageway, always just within the speed limit so as not to attract attention. Luca and Freya were in the back, doors locked, Luca's phone safely in the pocket of the small man with the evil eyes and the gun and the unoriginal name. The bigger one, who Shorty had called Tallboy, drove without a word. The radio was tuned to quiet classical music. Shorty glanced back at them from time to time. Luca ignored him. He was focusing all his thoughts on what to do next. Shorty had his sword stashed away somewhere. He had taken it carefully, clearly concerned it might send out another web to wrap them up, or something worse, but Luca knew he didn't need to worry. The sword was quiet and not responding to any signal Luca tried to send it.

He had no idea where they were being taken but it felt safe to assume Madoc would be waiting at the other end of the journey. He wondered if he might be killed straightaway. The two thugs who had captured them had rung somebody to let them know they had Freya, and Luca had caught a few snippets of the conversation. He had heard Shorty explain they had a boy who could do something completely freaky with a sword necklace, and then he had seen Shorty's face curl open into the widest grin ever. Clearly whoever was on the other end of the phone was mightily pleased to find out who else had been captured.

Freya's eyes were closed. She sat calmly with her hands folded in her lap, head drifting gently from side to side with the car's movement. Shorty's phone rang. Freya did not respond.

'Yeah, well on the way. We'll be in Canterbury in about an hour. See you at the meeting point. No, we're not being followed. Yes, I know what I'm doing.'

The call ended.

'Arrogant idiot,' he muttered, staring at the screen. 'Thinks he owns us, Tallboy.'

'Who? The policeman?'

'No, the other one he made me call. I think our Commissioner friend is keeping his head down. Anyway, that's enough. Don't let this pair hear anything they don't need to.'

We already have, thought Luca. So one way or another, he was going to Canterbury.

The car hummed along, the music soothing in spite of their predicament. Luca started to drift into sleep. It seemed like he hadn't slept properly in days. The music faded. He was dreaming. He was outside the car looking in at himself. Freya's eyes suddenly opened and fixed on him. He jumped back, because her eyes were completely black. He remembered how Freddie's eyes had looked when the Prince had spoken through him. This looked exactly the same.

'Don't be scared,' Freya said. 'I'm in your dream, Luca. I'm using dark magic to reach in and find you. Stay calm. We have to be ready to escape when we get to Canterbury.'

'How?' Luca said, and somehow he could speak out loud even though he was looking at himself fast asleep on the back seat.

'Madoc needs the blood. The pot is under the Black Prince's tomb. I don't know how he's going to get in but that's what he'll have to do. Then he needs me to say the reversal spell and release the Prince's soul. So I can't go down there. I just can't.'

'My friends will be there. I know they will. Between us we can stop Madoc. You won't have to go anywhere.'

'I hope you're right.'

She closed her eyes, and the link between them was lost. Luca's dream drifted off, as dreams always do, and now he was high above what he guessed was Canterbury cathedral. He sensed that there were ravens close by, and he also heard Madeleine calling to him, just as she had drawn him to the Tower. He saw her small frame walking across a moonlit square. She approached the great black bulk of the cathedral. He tried to call to her, to warn her of what was going to happen, but in this dream he had no voice. Then the car was crunching over gravel and Luca was awake. Tallboy switched off the engine. They had arrived.

'Get out,' ordered Shorty, reinforcing the point with a wave of his gun.

Luca and Freya climbed out of the car and stretched, taking it all in. They had parked close to the cathedral and it dominated the sky, blocking out most of the light, leaving them in deep shadow, which clearly suited their captors. The car lights had been turned off for the slow quiet crawl through the city's back streets. Shorty paused, as if waiting for instructions. Somebody whistled softly. Shorty nodded and pushed them roughly towards a low wall.

'That's close enough,' said a voice that Luca recognised.

'Gabriel,' he whispered. 'Bad guy. Madoc's man.'

'I'm going to run for it,' Freya replied.

'You don't stand a chance.'

'Worth the risk.'

'Really isn't.'

Gabriel stepped out of the shadows, pistol pointed directly at them. He looked at Luca with a calm, dispassionate stare.'

'Hello again, Mr Broom. Nice of you to join us.'

He moved aside. Madoc emerged, gripping Gwen's arm so tightly she was close to tears. Luca's heart sank. This was suddenly worse than he had feared.

'Excellent work, gentlemen. I imagine the commissioner has agreed a decent payment for your services.'

'You're John Madoc,' Shorty said. 'I'd know you anywhere.'

'Thank you,' Madoc replied, the smile fading. 'Your work is done. You may go.'

Tallboy stepped towards the car but Shorty stopped him with the palm of his hand.

'No, no. Not so fast. This changes everything. You've got billions, Madoc. This feels worth more than the fifty thousand that Johnson offered.'

'You aren't in any position to start negotiating,' Madoc whispered, looking less than pleased. He turned to Luca. 'I won't waste any time on small talk, Broom. You know how this is going to end. Hand over your sword, please.'

'I don't have it,' Luca replied.

'You're lying.'

'No, I'm not. Ask him.'

Luca nodded at Shorty, who seemed unsure what to do next. Gabriel made up his mind for him, swiftly closing the gap between them before checking his pockets. Shorty protested and Tallboy looked like he might decide to involve his fists in the argument, but the criminals instinctively recognised they were no match for Gabriel. The sword was passed to Madoc who studied it briefly before slipping into his jacket.

'You two are welcome to stay and help me. I will pay you for your extra time and inconvenience, of course.'

'What do we have to do?' Shorty asked.

'Not very much at all,' Madoc smiled. 'Wait here for some more children. Follow them into the cathedral. Then it might get interesting.'

'Will there be any more of that funny business like he did with the sword?'

'Oh, I do hope so, said Madoc. 'I really do.'

31

The day's dim light was fading so quickly, it was almost like someone was turning a dial. As they moved through the cathedral grounds, it became increasingly difficult to see where they were stepping, and on more than one occasion they tripped over half-buried headstones or uneven paths. They had to cross a gravel path and George winced at the loud crunching noises they made. So much for moving unnoticed.

Freddie was quiet, unwilling to respond to them. His collapse had been unnerving, and they moved with fresh urgency, unsure what to do or where to go but knowing that somewhere close, their missing friends might be danger.

The cathedral was open but there weren't many people around – just a handful of dark-eyed individuals, heads down, hands rammed into pockets, hunched against the cold. Nobody looked at them as they passed, and George relaxed a little.

Candles had been lit throughout the inside. The gentle yellow light played on the ancient stone walls, casting strange dancing shadows. It was less cold out of the wind, and George felt a sudden sense of calm. Their feet echoed softly. They paused, huddled together like pilgrims at the end of a long and terrible journey, like so many had done before them down the centuries. The light flecked across old military flags that hung from the walls, faded by time and war, and as they edged further into the cathedral, countless bishops and saints smiled down on them. The huge stone columns rose up above them like a whale's ribs. The ceiling arched impossibly overhead. In spite of everything, it was impossible not to be awed by the sheer overwhelming beauty of the place.

'Where's the tomb?' Carter asked, practical as ever.

'At the back. Follow me.'

George took the lead, remembering the way from his school visit. The few remaining visitors paid them no attention. Some were sat deep in thought and prayer. Others were wandering slowly around, looking up at the stained glass windows or down at the gravestones set into the floor.

Everything seems different, George thought. People are lost in their own worlds, or grieving for loved ones.

'I don't like how it feels,' he whispered. 'It's like looking at everything through a mirror.'

'The plague's changed them,' Jess replied. 'Made them think about the important stuff instead of worrying about whether their phones are cool or they've got enough likes on Instagram.'

'I was never that bothered by that kind of thing anyway.'

'Nor me.'

'You really like Luca, don't you? I mean, sorry to say anything. It's just that I've seen how you look at each other.'

197

'It's that obvious?'

'Yes.'

'I don't just like him, George. I love him. I'm really scared he didn't get into the tunnel fast enough. He could be a ghost now, wandering around somewhere. We'd never know.'

'I think he's okay. Don't ask me how I know. I just do.'

'Thanks, George.'

'Welcome.'

'I'm glad Ambrose brought you to Camelot.'

'So am I. Well, I think so, anyway.'

'I hate to break up the counselling session,' Carter growled, 'but I want to find Gwen.'

It didn't take long to find the tomb, at the far end of the cathedral, and they stood in silence, unsure what to do next. It was huge, the high iron bars surrounding it like a cage. A bronze image of the Black Prince lay across the stone sarcophagus. He seemed to be asleep, his fingertips rested lightly against each other. He didn't seem weighed down by his armour. In fact, eternity looked a comfortable place, with his feet rested on a small dog and a light smile across his face. His gloves, helmet, shield, tunic and scabbard were suspended over the tomb. It was an unsettling place, somehow peaceful and tense at the same time.

Carter reached through the bars and touched the metal.

'What are you doing?' George hissed.

'Just checking he's not alive. When we arrive, statues have a habit of waking up.'

'What will happen?' Madeleine asked. She looked anxiously at Freddie. 'Please don't change again. I don't like it.'

Freddie didn't reply and George could see how troubled he was. That was hardly a surprise considering what had happened. It was almost like the Black Prince was pulling him in piece by piece, dragging him closer.

'Are you okay?' Jess asked her brother. 'If you want to, we can go back outside.'

Freddie shook his head.

'He said the others were coming closer. He mentioned his sword. That's Gwen, isn't it? We have to be here.'

The air was still, a strange waiting for something, and for George an increasingly uneasy sense that this was all a really bad idea.

'Somebody do something,' he said, almost pleading with them to act.

'The writing,' Freddie replied. 'Look.'

He pointed at an inscription around the base of the tomb and began to read it out aloud.

'Such as thou art, sometime was I. Such as I am, such shalt thou be. I thought little on the hour of Death so long as I enjoyed breath. On earth I had great riches, land, houses, great treasure, horses, money and gold. But now a wretched captive am I, deep in the ground, lo here I lie. My beauty great, is all quite gone. My flesh is wasted to the bone.'

When he finished, Freddie closed his eyes. George held his breath, expecting the Black Prince to suddenly appear out of nowhere, but nothing happened.

'Nice speech,' said Carter, 'I guess millions of people must have read that out.'

'Yes,' Freddie replied, suddenly more alert and animated, 'but none of them had these.'

Freddie lifted up his sword. The blade was glowing in the dim light. All of the swords were doing the same.

'Going to be interesting trying to explain this if anybody sees,' Carter said. 'It's really hot!'

He flicked his sword out as if it was a firework ready to go off. The blade was glowing all the way to the handle. 'You did this, Freddie? Just by saying a few words?'

'It's a spell, you idiot. Been here all this time. The swords have magic in them. Do I have to explain everything?'

Carter looked like he was about to tell Freddie exactly what he thought of that, but he didn't get the chance. Something was happening under their feet.

'Did you feel that?' Madeleine asked.

'Yes,' replied Freddie, still pointing his now white-hot sword at the tomb. 'The floor moved.'

He was right. The ancient floor of the cathedral had definitely shifted a little, like an animal sighing in its sleep. Then it happened again and the bronze knight started to lift up. The Black Prince was now at an angle. They backed away from the bars, which were bowed and stretched apart. A small child could now easily slip between them, and when the floor lurched again and the gap between the bars widened further, that's exactly what Freddie did.

'No,' George shouted. 'You don't know if it's safe.'

'No, I don't,' Freddie replied as he put both hands on the knight's chest, 'but I don't think we're supposed to just stand there doing nothing.'

Another groan and shift, and now the prince was at forty five degrees, his feet almost touching the cracked flagstones. Clouds of dust lifted up and the huge stone slabs of the tomb began to lean outwards. The swords weren't just glowing now – they were humming in unison, an odd low drone of a noise that was getting louder by the second.

'I really don't like this!' Madeleine shouted. She buried her face in Hug-a-Bug.

'Nor me,' Jess agreed.

'We're going to be in serious trouble when someone sees the mess,' said Carter.

'No we won't,' said Freddie. He pointed over their heads. 'Look.'

They were surrounded by some kind of shimmering bubble that stretched completely around them and the tomb. Beyond it, the cathedral was untouched. A man strolled past, humming quietly. He paid them no attention whatsoever.

'He can't see us,' George said. 'Maybe it looks completely normal out there.'

It certainly wasn't normal inside the bubble, because now a terrible groan built from somewhere and the floor around the tomb began to swell, like a boil that was ready to pop. The stone flags stretched and lifted as if they were made of rubber, and the Black Prince rose up to the vertical, his feet still resting on the little dog, his eyes thankfully still closed.

They edged closer, wary of the statue. Freddie peered around the back.

'There we go,' he said.

Where the tomb had stood, there was now a jagged hole in the ground, and steps leading down into the darkness below. Their swords faded back to cold metal and there was suddenly deathly silence.

'I guess we have to go down there,' Carter said, 'but I don't mind saying that it looks really scary.'

'Then it's good we've got each other,' replied Jess, taking Madeleine's hand. 'Follow me. If Luca's down there, I'm going to find him.'

'Same with Gwen,' added Carter. 'Let's do this.'

They descended one at a time, George bringing up the rear. He took one last look around before he did, still struggling to comprehend any of it.

***

Just out of sight of the tomb, across the expanse of old floor where a single candle gently burned, Madoc nodded to Gabriel. Luca squirmed and fought but there

202

was no way to escape Gabriel's hand clamped over his mouth, especially with one arm bent up behind his back. Gwen and Freya were more compliant, allowing themselves to be shoved forwards by Shorty and Tallboy. The heat from their swords had been so intense Madoc had taken them out of his pocket and held them at arm's length to avoid getting burned, but the heat had now died away. He put them back, ignoring the slightly uncomfortable feeling they produced, as if the swords were angry. It was entirely possible the damn things could think. Their power unsettled him. The first chance he got, Madoc planned to bury them in the deepest darkest hole he could find, preferably with all the others' swords.

'This is making me nervous,' Shorty said. 'Not sure I want to go down there.'

'Then you don't get the extra money.'

'You going back on a promise?'

'Are you giving me a reason to?'

'Not yet,' Shorty said. 'Just like to know what we're up against.'

'A bunch of children, if you hadn't noticed.'

'Children who can do real magic.'

'Shut up and get down the steps. And go quietly.'

Madoc didn't trust the two hired thugs who had delivered him Broom and the girl, and if they became a nuisance, he might need Gabriel to dispose of them, but until then he was content to let them tag along. The big one in particular might be useful in a fight. It would depend how they coped with the magic he hoped to unleash. It might be enough to drive them insane.

He guessed that they had been able to see what was happening because of the children's swords, and that nobody else in the cathedral could, so it was safe to assume they wouldn't be followed. It was still all working out just as the spell book had said it would.

32

It was surprisingly warm down in the tunnel that led from the steps. The air shifted around like something breathing, and the faint smell of stale cheese clung to their skin and clothes. George wrinkled his nose as he walked, his eyes darting around, checking for danger.

They were heading downwards on a gentle gradient. Each turn took them a little further below the cathedral, and George had to stop himself from imagining the massive weight of it.

It's been there a thousand years, he thought. I don't suppose it's going to suddenly break through into here now.

But the idea had taken hold and he couldn't quite shake it off. Jess moved up next to him.

'Relax,' she said. 'Stay calm. We're going to be okay, you know?'

He didn't know any such thing, and there was something about the way she spoke that made him think neither did she, but he said nothing. Instead, he smiled in the half light and kept walking. The feeling of crushing dread grew stronger with each step. Nobody spoke. They were hunched over and tense, moving furtively, the air increasingly hot and dusty. George coughed and the sound ricocheted around the enclosed space.

'Keep the noise down,' Carter growled, and George heard real fear in his voice, which didn't help.

The tunnel drifted this way and that for around fifty metres. The stale cheese smell was stronger. Suddenly, without warning, candles flared around them. Ahead of them was a room with a high arched ceiling. Hundreds of clay pots were littered across the floor. They moved in gently, careful not to disturb any of them. Before anybody had a chance to speak, shouting erupted from behind them.

'Don't any of you move!'

George froze. He was staring at a tough looking man with a pistol.

'Gabriel,' whispered Jess. 'He works for Madoc.'

'Well remembered,' chuckled Madoc as he strolled into the room. Then Luca, Gwen and a girl were dragged in by two other men, one huge with a scar down his face, the other small and weasel-eyed.

'All back together,' Madoc said. 'Lovely. And thank you so much for opening the tomb for me. Just as I hoped you would.'

***

Gabriel twisted Luca's arm further up his back. His shoulder joint burned with the agony of it but he managed to stop himself from screaming. No way was he going to give Madoc the satisfaction of hearing that. Instead, he delivered as many swear words as he could remember, in as loud a voice as he could manage. It helped. Then he smiled at his friends and told them he was okay. Gwen did the same before they were silenced by a flick of Gabriel's pistol against his skull.

'Thank you for showing us the way in,' Madoc said. 'It was too easy, really. Just wait for you all to turn up, with your fancy swords and your teamwork thing. I have to say, even I was impressed by the way it worked. I had guessed the tomb might collapse but the way the Black Prince stood up, that was real theatre.'

He was really enjoying himself, playing to his captive audience. Luca glanced at George. He didn't have a good feeling about how Madoc would react when he knew who he was. Madoc was clearly demented, so far removed from sanity that the slightest thing might be enough to tip him further into violence.

'Don't you all look suitably surprised and terrified,' Madoc said. His grin was getting bigger by the second. His eyes flashed in the candlelight and he actually waved at them, like a jovial uncle welcoming them for Christmas.

'And now we're all together, let's do the introductions. I feel like we've been here before, except of course last time the surroundings were rather better.' Madoc spat on the floor. 'And thanks to you, Broom, nothing more than a burned out pile.'

'I think that might have more to do with you wanting to kill everybody,' Luca muttered. He was too hot and tired to care any more.

'Insolent bravery will get you absolutely nowhere, boy. It's over this time. I'm going to have the devil's blood. I'm going to be king.'

Madoc leaned forwards, taking his time, fixing each of them with that snake-like stare. Madeleine whimpered and cuddled in close to Jess. Madoc's gaze lingered over George. A look of disbelief crossed his face, quickly followed by anger so dark and terrible that Luca wouldn't have been surprised if flames had roared out of Madoc's mouth.

'You...you look very familiar,' Madoc whispered. 'Same dark hair, thin mouth, arrogant eyes.'

George smiled, and to Luca it was the bravest thing he had ever seen.

'Thanks for the compliments,' he said. 'Just a pity my dad can't be here to say such nice things about me.'

Madoc ripped the sword from around George's neck. The stone glittered in the candlelight.

'Randall's boy? He had a son that I never knew about?'

He spun around and hurled the sword straight at Gabriel, bouncing off his chest onto the floor.

'I'm sorry, Mr Madoc,' Gabriel said, but Luca had never heard anybody say it with less meaning. 'This should have been known.'

'It should have been known? It should have been stopped! This brat should have been drowned at birth! How many other secret children are there out there?'

Madoc grabbed George's arm and wrenched him up. 'Brothers? Sisters? Tell me!'

George said nothing. He returned Madoc's stare, unblinking and calm. Madoc let go.

'Well, it doesn't matter. I've got you now,' but there was a new edge of something close to fear in Madoc's voice and Luca knew the others had sensed it too. They were all focused and alert. Madoc kicked the wall and winced in pain. He was already limping, but now he had to almost hobble back to where Gabriel was standing.

'Hurt yourself?' George asked. 'Is your scary friend with the gun going to kiss it better?'

'Not a good idea,' Luca muttered.

'So he shoots me now rather than in five minutes? I can't say the options are exactly wonderful.'

Madoc ordered Gabriel to get the rest of the swords. Just for a few seconds, Luca hoped that they would all suddenly come alive. He watched the blades for any hint of heat or light but there was nothing. Gabriel held the swords easily, with no sign of discomfort or distress and Luca knew it was not going to happen. Gabriel handed them to Madoc, who studied them silently before putting them in his pocket. Then Madoc yanked Freya painfully into the centre of the room.

'One wrong move from any of you will be your last,' Madoc said. 'And for the benefit of those of you who haven't met her, this is Freya Morgan. Her dad was also killed by Gabriel at the Tower. Remember him? The fat man who didn't look carefully when you rats scrambled out of the sewers.'

Freya glared at him with pure hatred.

'No funny business,' he growled. 'I know what you're capable of.'

Then Madoc turned to Luca.

'And you, Broom, should have killed me when you had the chance, but you didn't have the stomach for it.'

Luca's heart was beating so loudly, he wouldn't have been surprised if they all could hear it. If he thought he could make it, he would have launched himself at Madoc. It would have been futile, of course. Gabriel was ready for any such attack. They were utterly beaten.

'Enough of this stupid chat,' Madoc continued, a new edge to his voice. 'I can't pretend to be nice to any of you for much longer.'

He laughed at his own joke. The laugh was unpleasant, like burnt toast being cut with a rusty saw.

'Let's keep this simple. Do anything you shouldn't, Gabriel kills you. Attack me, Gabriel kills you. Try anything at all...well, Gabriel kills you.'

Luca's leg was aching horribly and he moved slightly. His foot bumped against a pot. It toppled over with a crash. A pale smoky cloud drifted out, faint and barely there. Luca heard a quiet sigh. The smoke passed across his face. He breathed it in and he shivered because he realised it wasn't smoke. It was somehow a person, and that person had reached into his brain and shown him everything they had been, before they had died.

'Who was it?' shouted Madoc. 'Tell me, Broom. Who did you feel?'

Madoc's voice was distorted and painful to hear, and Luca stumbled back into one of the others. His throat was constricted and he couldn't breathe. He gulped and coughed, desperate to get any of the foul cheesy air into his lungs, to remove the feeling of being mingled up with someone else.

'A girl,' he croaked, not even that aware he was speaking out loud. 'Not very old. They said she was a witch. They killed her and stuck her soul in the pot.'

The smoke was gone. He could breathe again. Somebody took his shoulders. It was George, staring anxiously at him.

'You okay? You really slammed into me.'

'Just a girl,' interrupted Madoc. 'Nobody important. Don't anybody touch another pot.'

'What just happened?' Luca said, rubbing his eyes. He wanted every bit of whatever it was gone from his skin.

'The soul of a long dead innocent,' Madoc replied. 'Killed by superstitious fools and trapped in that pot for all of eternity. Well, at least until your clumsy feet released her. Now move over here, carefully. Now!'

Luca knew Madoc was right. He had felt it in him, known exactly what it was – all that was left of the girl, no more than a memory, scrunched up like paper, full of pain and fear, desperately wanting to be released but also overwhelmingly sad because the girl knew that was

211

it. Now that the smoke had faded away, the girl was gone, forever. There was space on the floor to sit down, and suddenly Luca wanted to more than anything else. He was exhausted. His eyes were sore and gritty. His head hurt and his mouth tasted like old socks. And the smell of cheese was worse than ever. He squatted on the stone flags.

'Get up, Broom,' Madoc said.

'Make me.'

Nobody spoke for a few seconds, then Carter sat down next to Luca.

'Can I join you?'

'Feel free.'

'Get up, both of you!'

Madoc was angry now. His voice was a little higher.

'Do one, Madoc,' Carter said without looking.

Then the others did the same. They sat in a sullen bunch with their eyes down. The room was stuffy and getting warmer by the second. Luca's hands were slick with sweat. None of them were getting out of here alive, he guessed.

'Let's get on with this,' said Madoc, rubbing his leg.

He clicked his fingers and Gabriel shoved the gun barrel into Freya's back, pushing her into the middle of the chamber. Madoc took something out of his pocket and held it up for them all to see.

'Merlin's spell book. You brats might have ruined everything last time, but there's no way you can now. The book is very clear on how all of this would play out, so it's time for some witchcraft. Your new friend is going to find the Black Prince's pot and recite the spell. She'll bring him back to life.'

'I won't do it,' Freya said.

'Well, you will,' Madoc replied. 'And here's why. The next time you refuse, Gabriel shoots that one.' He pointed at Madeleine, who immediately began to cry. 'After that, each refusal will result in another death, until there's just you left.'

Luca started to protest.

'Save your anger, Broom,' Madoc said. 'There's nothing you can do. I'll let you live, and you can deal with the grief for the rest of your miserable life. So what's it going to be, witch?'

Freya's head bowed.

'Don't do it,' Gwen called. 'Let him kill us all. Anything to stop him.'

'You really are starting to annoy me,' said Madoc. 'And I once thought you might be good enough to inherit it all. That was a serious mistake.'

'I can't let him kill you,' Freya said. 'I'll do what he wants.'

'A wise decision. Now do it.'

Freya started to drift among the pots, her fingers trailing across the lids. The gentle sighing of warm air mixed with the sound of their breathing. It was as if the chamber itself knew what was going to happen. Some of the pots were so old they had already cracked open. There were no souls left in those, and Freya ignored them. She leaned down to inspect one. It was short and squat, and covered in strange scratches. Then she shook her head and moved on. Luca wasn't sure if she was playing for time, but it was mesmerising to watch, the way she paused and then swayed, stroking the ancient clay, probing with her mind. She examined and rejected more and more pots. Madoc was growing increasingly agitated.

'Don't mess with me, girl. Just show me the Black Prince.'

Freya ignored him and kept moving around the chamber. A few more pots were checked. Then, almost like an afterthought, she stopped next to a tall slim pot. It was utterly unremarkable.

'That one,' she said dully. 'He's all yours.'

Madoc must have been holding his breath, because a strange gurgling noise echoed around the chamber as he breathed in and out. He almost ran across the cluttered room, not caring who he kicked or stamped on as he did. He was utterly focused on the pot. He skidded to a halt and reached down, his hands hovering over it, almost unable to bring himself to actually touch it.

'Get on with it,' Carter groaned.

Madoc glared at him and did exactly that. He picked up the pot, treasuring it like a parent holding a newborn baby.

'Say the spell,' he whispered. 'Say it now.'

Freya's eyes glistened with tears and her lips were trembling.

'Say it, girl!'

'I can't. I promised my nan I would never, ever say it.'

The tears were splashing onto her cheeks and her shoulders heaved with each gulping cry. Madoc stalked towards her, snarling as he went.

'You've got five seconds until Gabriel kills the first one. Say the spell.'

'I...I...'

'Five. Four. Three. Say it. Two.'

Freya looked desperately at Madeleine, herself in tears and shaking with fear.

'I'm sorry. I really am.'

'One. Over to you, Gabriel.'

Luca closed his eyes. He saw his mum and dad, and he thought of how much he loved them, and how much he loved all of his friends. He wanted to hold Madeleine close. He hoped it would be quick. It was unfair, the way it had ended.

And that was when the ravens arrived.

33

Dozens of the birds swirled into the room, filling it with noise, chaos and clouds of feathers, and extinguishing most of the candles. They all ducked down against the storm. Gabriel's pistol fired in the darkness and a screech of pain made Luca's heart flip, but it was a raven that fell to the ground, not Madeleine. Madoc was shouting curses. The pot tumbled from his hands but it didn't break. He tried to reach it but he was forced back by the birds.

Gabriel fired again. More birds dropped dead. Then they turned on him like sharks going for the kill and he disappeared underneath a mass of squirming, flapping bodies.

Luca pushed away a raven that seemed intent on ripping his hair out. The bird seemed to recognise him, squawked what could easily have been an apology, then aimed at Tallboy. The huge man was forced down to his knees by sheer pressure of the attack, as was his shorter colleague. It was total mayhem. Luca was suddenly eyeball to eyeball with Bran. He clicked and clacked and pecked at Luca's ears.

'How did you know?' Luca shouted. 'Oh, never mind, it doesn't matter. I'm really glad you're here, mate. Thanks!'

In the space of a few seconds they had gone from disaster to something that was looking increasingly like triumph. He ruffled Bran's head feathers and rubbed his beak for good measure. The noise was dying down. The ravens had subdued each of their attackers. Madoc and his men sat in an untidy huddle, arms crossed and heads down.

But, in the noise and chaos, it had been too easy to miss somebody doing something unexpected. That somebody was Freddie. He had crawled along the floor, keeping low on his elbows and knees. He had separated himself from the group. Now, he stood up. He was holding the pot and his eyes gleamed black, like freshly poured tar.

'Freddie, no,' shouted Luca. 'Put it down.'

'What's he doing?' George asked.

'I am doing what needs to be done,' Freddie said, except the voice was not his. It was the Black Prince, just as it had been at the Tower.

Everything seemed to slow down, as if the whole planet had shifted slightly on its axis. Luca felt a horrible sickening lurch in his gut. Freddie raised an arm and swept it left and right. A horrible noise enveloped them and sparks flew from his fingers.

'That's dark magic,' Freya screamed. 'How does he know it?'

Even the ravens were affected. They tried to fly but seemed disoriented, bumping into the walls and ceiling of the room. They screamed in confusion and pain. Bran slumped down next to Luca. The bird's eyes were dull. His beak gaped. Something was badly wrong.

The Black Prince smiled.

'I will be free,' he said.

Words came quickly from his lips, jumbles of rhyme and song, a strange ancient mixture of sounds.

'Oh no,' Freya gasped. 'He's saying the release spell.'

Luca could only watch in horror. The thing that had been Freddie was swaying like a sapling in a storm. His eyes were now closed. The pot was above his head. The lid slipped, then settled back on top. He was chanting the spell with increased urgency. The Black Prince was completely in control.

Then he dropped the pot. It fell too slowly, like a balloon drifting down, or a feather. Nobody tried to grab it. Things were too far gone for that, and their limbs were somehow heavier than they should be, and their brains dulled. This time, when the lid slipped, it separated from the pot. A thin smear of smoke came away, like an afterthought, but the smoke thickened and the lid tumbled faster. It smashed silently into dust.

The pot hit the ground a moment later and exploded. There was no sound, and that was more terrible, because such a violent explosion of light and dust needed noise to make it real. It might as well have happened in the freezing vacuum of space because the room was no longer a place where the normal rules of gravity and air applied. It had become something incredible and impossible, and they were in there watching it all unfold in front of their eyes.

They were covered by a thick cloud of dust that immediately choked them with its stinging bitterness, turning their throats to sandpaper and making their eyes stream hot tears. They staggered around trying to get away but the dust was everywhere. Then as fast as it had filled the chamber, the dust was gone. It was one of the strangest things that Luca had ever seen – one moment the air thick with it, then as if someone had switched off a light, the dust was sucked down into a tiny crack on the floor, so small it had been unnoticed, until then.

'Freddie!' Jess gasped, eyes wide, fixed on her brother. 'What were you saying? Where did you learn that?'

Freddie's eyes were clear again. He looked as if he was waking from a coma. There was no understanding there. His mouth hung slackly open. He blinked, trying to focus.

'I...he...he was inside my head again...I couldn't do anything...what did I do?'

'You broke the pot,' continued Jess, stating the obvious, as if she couldn't believe it. 'You said the spell. Oh, Freddie, you said the spell!'

'The Black Prince made him do it,' said Madeleine and her hand searched for anybody who might want to hold it. Freya did. Her face was pale. Her eyes were narrow. She was tensed, like a marathon runner at the exact second when the gun is fired and the race begins.

'Yeah,' she whispered. 'That was the spell. The one I was taught as a kid. The one I had to make sure was never ever used.'

Freddie turned to her. Luca couldn't imagine anybody ever looking more alone.

'I didn't want to. I had no choice. He was too strong. He used me.'

'Too late to worry about it now,' Freya said. 'Look.'

The crack in the floor was bigger than Luca remembered it being a few seconds ago. And then it was bigger still, like a dark spreading stain. A tiny pinprick of light blossomed at its middle. The light grew brighter and began to rise up in a vertical beam. It was quickly two metres tall, almost to the ceiling. It was more than just light. It had solidity to it, a yellow shimmering something that might have been arms or legs, or perhaps a head, and then that was exactly it – the light faded to leave a figure, as if a camera had flashed and they were looking at the image it had left behind. It was a man in dark polished armour, with a face like a hawk. His hands gripped a sword that was nearly as long as he was tall, and he stared at them with eyes so black and cold, Luca's legs seemed to turn to water.

'The spell is reversed,' the Black Prince said. 'It was most fortunate that I was able to find such an amenable mind in which to hide. Fortunate and wonderful. Oh, how many years have I waited for this?' He stretched, rising up even taller. 'The witch has failed. Is she here to see my victory?'

He cast his gaze across them, like an executioner deciding whose neck will be next on his block. He stopped at Freya. Those cold eyes widened and the slightest trace of a smile flickered at the corners of his mouth.

'Not her, but one who looks very much like her. You, child. Step up. Tell me your name.'

Freya pushed Madeleine behind her.

'You know who I am,' she said.

'Yes, of course,' the Prince said, and the smile was gone, if it was ever there at all. 'The daughter of the daughter of the daughter...there are too many to count, but you still have the look and the odour of the witch that you are.'

Freya shoved Madeleine further back. The younger girl fell against Luca. She wrapped herself around him and buried her face into his chest.

'I'm now very very scared,' she mumbled.

'So am I,' he replied.

The Black Prince turned to him.

'And who are you?'

Luca swallowed hard, gripping onto Madeleine.

'Luca Pendragon Broom,' he said, and he hated the tremble in his voice.

The Prince leaned forward. One eyebrow raised up. The slight smile was back.

'A Plantagenet, eh? One of my own, in league with the witches. This is a terrible time into which I am reborn.'

Nobody moved. The Prince stalked around them, leaning in close, sizing them up, sniffing them, reaching out to touch them but not quite letting his fingers make contact. He stopped next to Freddie.

'Yes, most fortunate. The moment I sensed you, my young friend, I knew I had a chance. You were at the Tower. You were near my armour and the sword made for my ancestor by the wizard Merlin. That was all I needed - the link to the past and a brain with enough natural magic to let me in. Oh, it was so exciting to see through your eyes that day, to smell the world, to escape for a few precious seconds the awful blackness of that pot. And then the connection was lost, but not entirely. Some part of me stayed in you. You've felt it. I know you have. All I had to do was push myself into your mind when you arrived in this room and then get you to recite the words. It worked! I am free!'

He moved on to Gwen, studying her very carefully.

'You wear the very sword of which I speak. Who are you?'

'My name is Gwen and you have to listen to me.' She gestured at her father. 'That man is evil. He wanted you brought back so he could take some of your blood. There is another part of the spell that says if that happens, he will become king.'

This seemed to first amuse the Prince, then anger him as he realised Gwen was serious. He turned his fierce gaze on Madoc.

'You would presume such a thing?'

Madoc said nothing. He was now just a cowering wreck, no longer in charge. The Prince shook his head.

'Pathetic. I can see I have nothing to fear from him.'

'How did you know the reversal spell?' Freya asked, still hiding the shivering Madeleine behind her. 'Nobody knows the words except witches. Nobody.'

The Black Prince smiled like a wolf.

'Nobody except a victim of the dark magic that imprisoned me. I felt all the thoughts and memories of your ancestor as she sucked my soul into the pot. From that moment on, I knew the words. I needed a connection with someone to speak them aloud. I despaired that I would find such a connection until that day not so long ago. I knew then that my time of imprisonment was coming to an end. More than six hundred years! Can you imagine what it has been like? Of course you cannot. Now I will at last claim the crown that was stolen from me. How the false rulers will feel my wrath!'

Luca caught a blur of movement off to his side. He turned just as Madoc lunged at the Prince, and even though the knight was more ghost than man, he was solid enough to be hurt by the tip of the sword in Madoc's outstretched hand. He fell forwards through the half-smoke, half flesh. His fall seemed slower than it should, because the Prince's half-formed body partially stopped him, then he was through and sprawling on the dusty floor. He lay still for a few seconds, and nobody moved. Then Madoc turned to them, and he was grinning, and the sword dripped something dark and sticky.

'Fooled by my scared little rabbit act, eh?' he said. 'You idiots. I'm not so pathetic now, am I? The Devil's blood is mine.'

The ghostly outline of the Prince had broken up as Madoc fell through it, but it quickly reformed, and Luca saw something that had not been there before – a dark smudge on the Prince's neck that could have been a bruise, but bruises don't spread that quickly and they certainly don't bleed.

'He...cut me,' the Prince moaned. He reached up to the wound and his fingers came away covered in blood. 'That can't happen. It's impossible, unless...'

'I did it with a sword made by the same family of witches as the one who trapped you in that pot,' grinned Madoc, and he lifted the blade to his lips. A single drop of the dark sticky blood formed at the tip. It hung there, almost too thick to fall, but it was heavy and there was dark magic at work, and so the drop did fall, and it fell into Madoc's mouth.

'I've tasted the blood of the kings and queens who lived and died with the Devil inside them. The blood of all the Plantagenets who worshipped Arthur as if he was some kind of god. And now it's my blood. At last, the Madocs will take what has always been ours. In the name of my ancestor Sir Mordred, I take the crown.'

'What evil is this?' the Prince gasped. The dark bloom was spreading across his chest like a rash. 'He has hurt me...he has taken the blood!'

He touched the wound. Sticky blood spread out over his hand. It could have been thick jam, the way it oozed and dripped. He didn't seem to notice. He was too enraged and too focused on the object of his anger. Madoc shrank back. His sword flopped against his chest, leaving a single blob of the jam-blood on his jacket.

'You would dare to attack me? You would presume to defeat me? You would entertain ideas of taking the Crown? Well. You will see what a true king can do.'

The Prince raised his arms up high and began to chant in the same strange language that had come from Freddie, except this time the words came out in a growl, with real menace, as if the words themselves were weapons.

'He's using a spell I don't know,' Freya said. 'This could be really bad. We should get out of here.'

Everybody seemed to have had the same idea. They all turned for the tunnel at the same time. The Prince swept a hand down and thick iron bars slid out of nowhere, blocking their path. The ravens screeched in fear. Shorty yelped and jumped back, rubbing his shoulder where one of the bars had hit him on its way down.

The Prince continued to speak, the chanting getting louder and more aggressive. All of his attention was now focused on Madoc, who backed away, eyes wide, hands held up in self-defence. Another sweep of the Prince's arm caused Freya to collapse. She lay motionless at his feet and Luca had no idea whether she was dead or simply unconscious.

'Now feel the pain,' the Prince said.

34

The Black Prince tipped back his head and roared. The noise was unbearable. They covered their ears against it but it was no good. The noise was not of the world. It came from somewhere else, and it hammered through skin and bone so that their eardrums vibrated painfully and their teeth shivered in their gums.

'Make him stop,' shouted Madeleine. She was crying. She had dropped Hug-a-Bug. He lay forgotten in the dust. The sound was everything. It was as if there had never been anything but that sound, and there would only be that sound for the rest of forever. Luca closed his eyes, but that somehow made it worse. At least if he looked at his friends, he didn't feel quite so alone.

Their faces betrayed the pain and fear. Even Carter couldn't pretend this wasn't a big deal. His hands were clamped over the sides of his head, the skin over his knuckles stretched with the effort of blocking out the noise. He looked at Luca. We can't do anything, that look meant. We've taken on more than we can handle. The sound was suddenly even louder, and Luca knew he was going to pass out. He actually hoped he would, because then the sound might leave him alone.

Madoc screamed and doubled over in agony. Gabriel, Tallboy and Shorty all did the same. The Prince was focusing his attack on them. They writhed and squirmed, begging him to stop whatever it was that he was doing to them. It seemed to go on forever.

Then it was over, replaced by a silence even more terrible than what had come before it, and the heavy thud, thud, thud of Luca's heartbeat that drummed through his skull. Madoc and his men fell face down, gasping for breath.

'And now you will die,' the Prince said, lifting up his hands once more, bringing them together like he was about to start praying. The words started again, horrible, rasping, evil words. Madoc clutched his chest.

Luca watched, horrified, knowing there was nothing any of them could do to stop it, and although he hated Madoc, he felt a sudden stab of sympathy for what the man was going through. He looked at Gwen. She was crying, holding on to Carter, reaching out towards the man who was still her father.

Then Luca noticed something else. Thin wisps of smoke were starting to lift off the Prince's armour, like a blown out match. He wasn't sure the smoke was real or just his brain trying to unscramble itself, but there was suddenly more smoke; a lot more.

Freya shifted ever so slightly, just at the edge of his vision. Her eyelids were flickering like paper in a strong wind, and her lips were silently mouthing. Something was definitely happening to the Prince. The smoke was thicker, and there must have been heat, because suddenly he lifted an arm. He stared, confused.

'What sorcery is this?' the Prince snarled.

'I think we're just about to find out,' muttered Carter. His eyes were blood-shot and he was shaking, but his usual defiance was rapidly coming back. He pointed at the Prince. 'You're toast, mate.'

The Prince cocked his head to one side, clearly with no comprehension of what Carter had said or meant. Freya's fingers were moving rapidly, like she was playing an invisible piano, and Luca realised she was throwing out some serious dark magic of her own. The smoke around the Prince's arms thickened and a tiny spark of flame burst across his armour. He screamed and waved his arms around, but the flame was spreading. He lost his balance and crashed down among the pots. Freya was on her feet in an instant. Her hands formed into claws and she thrust them out like weapons. At the same time she shouted out line after line of the strange otherworldly language,

'No!' he screamed. 'Not that! I will not go back into the pot!'

Freya wasn't giving up, even though a counter-attack spell caused her to stumble and almost fall. She kept up the barrage of words, her hands jabbing at the Prince, forcing him down onto his knees. He picked up fragments of pot and threw them at Freya. She ducked. It seemed to give the Prince a chance. He threw a few more and began his own chant. Freya continued, this time raising her voice above a whisper, speaking quickly as if desperate to get to the end, but the Prince was smiling and Luca could see why. The flames were shrinking back. The smoke was clearing. The spell was failing.

'I curse this land and all who live in it to eternal night and terrible cold. All the wonders of your age swept away. You shall know what it was to live in my time. And the words on my tomb will be carved across your souls as you feel the pain I've felt all these years.'

His voice rose again into that awful painful roar, and they all fell back in agony except for Freya who seemed to find the strength for one last effort. The Prince clutched his throat. The flames consumed him, leaving a swirling cloud of smoke that spun like a miniature tornado up into the air and then vanished into a small pale pot at the back of the room. Freya ran forwards and slammed down a lid. Then she collapsed, her breathing ragged, her forehead touching the floor in complete and utter exhaustion.

'You did it,' Jess shouted, lifting her up, helping her stand. 'You beat him. You star.'

'He did it first,' croaked Freya. She pointed up at the ceiling. 'I can't stop his curse.'

A crack slowly opened up above them like a fractured bone. The whole place shifted and groaned. They were all covered in thick dust and total darkness. It was impossible to tell which scream belonged to who, and Luca fought off a flurry of ravens' wings and claws as, in their panic, they attacked anything.

'Make them stop, Bran!' he shouted, but there was no way of making himself heard.

A torch flicked on, the beam cutting through the dust, showing him the way towards the exit. The iron bars were gone, vanished with their maker. Gabriel pushed him into a rapidly crumbling wall, dragging Madoc with him, holding the torch out straight to guide the way, no longer interested in anything but getting himself and his boss out of there.

'Time to be somewhere else, Tallboy,' he heard Shorty say, and they followed Gabriel and Madoc into the tunnel just as a large chunk of ceiling crashed down around them. Another thick cloud of dust filled the air, but by some miracle Gabriel was thrown off balance and he dropped the torch. Luca snatched it up.

'Keep it as a souvenir,' Gabriel snarled, then he was gone.

Luca cried out as more chunks of stone rained down. One bounced painfully off his back. Another scraped his elbow. The groaning of the walls and floor told him they had seconds before the whole place collapsed in on itself. He flashed the torch around, picking each of them out, guiding them to the exit, and like flour covered zombies they stumbled and coughed their way to him.

'Faster,' he urged. 'Come on!'

They were going to make it. Madeleine was the last to pass him. Then she stopped, turned and ran back into the shattered room.

'I've lost Hug-a-Bug,' she wailed, scrabbling at the rubble with her bare hands. 'Where is he?'

'Leave him, Madeleine,' Luca called. 'It's too late.'

She showed no sign of having heard him. She carried on searching. Luca was frozen to the spot, unable to move. Then, it was as if time slowed down, because he could see clearly what was going to happen but he was powerless to stop it.

'Found him,' Madeleine said, holding up the filthy tattered ladybird just as another horrible groan ripped across the ceiling, and the whole lot began to collapse.

No, thought Luca. This can't be happening.

Then Freddie jumped forwards. He tumbled over the rubble, one arm up to shield him from the lumps coming down. Madeleine looked at him, eyes wide with fear, Hug-a-Bug clutched to her chest.

'I found him, Freddie,' she repeated, and Luca's heart flipped.

'Well done,' Freddie said.

He grabbed Madeleine and shoved her towards the others. She fell into Jess's arms. Then the remaining ceiling gave and Freddie disappeared in a choking, smothering cloud of thick grey dust.

35

Freddie's gone.

That was the only thought running through Luca's head as he staggered along the tunnel, repeating over and over and over.

Freddie's gone.

Jess was next to him, and he was glad it was dark because he didn't want to see her eyes. He pushed on, the rumble of collapsing masonry a constant reminder of what had just happened and what was still happening. He risked a look over his shoulder. The tunnel was falling in. He could feel the pressure building behind them, like a tidal wave.

They reached the steps and somehow all managed to get up out of the tunnel just as it completely collapsed. The statue of the Prince leaned over them. It shifted and moved against its unstable foundation. They pushed through the bent and twisted railings and rolled away. The Prince and the remnants of his tomb disappeared through the gaping hole in the floor, the noise like a bomb going off, the clouds of smoke and dust spewing upwards like an erupting volcano.

Nothing seemed real. Luca wiped his eyes, unable to focus, painfully blinking away the grit and sediment that was all around them. The walls and grand columns of the cathedral were shifting. The immense stained glass windows seemed to be melting. It was all coming apart.

His ears were blocked with dust, and the sound of the collapse was dulled down to a series of low booms. The others were struggling to stand, each of them screaming silently, arms reaching for each other, panic and fear etched across their faces.

He saw Gwen helping Carter to his feet, and that at least felt good, because if they were going to die here, those two should be together.

You love her, Luca thought. Even if it's only once in your life, find a way to tell her.

Freya, the witch girl who he hardly knew and who was still a stranger to the others, was huddled alone, eyes fixed on him, and he remembered the promise he made her. She was among friends.

George was holding onto a swaying statue of an angel, his face white with dust except for a startling red gash across his forehead. There was so much Luca still had to say to him, to tell him about his dad, to just sit and chat, and there had never seemed to be any time and now never would be.

And Jess was suddenly close by, her hand suddenly in his, her mind reaching for him so that all of the pain she was feeling swept through him and it was too awful to bear. She stood tall and silent, her eyes gleaming, knowing every thought that was flashing through him, and he knew at that moment he would never love anybody in the way he loved her, together in the terrible cauldron of smoke and fire and fear.

'I'm sorry,' he shouted. 'I should have saved him.'

All of Jess's thoughts were mixed up with his own, as if their voices had become one.

There was nothing you could do...I love you...Freddie's gone...I'm sorry...we failed...I love you, too...

There was no way out. Everything was a mess of tumbling masonry and thick dust clouds. Exposed wires sparked into small fires that quickly spread. Shattered timbers crackled and burned, adding choking black smoke to the developing catastrophe. A pipe suddenly burst, drenching them in freezing water. It was impossible to see. They had no way of knowing which way to run. High above them, the cathedral tower groaned and shifted, like a wounded animal breathing its last.

'It's all going to come down,' Carter screamed. 'We've got to get out!'

But there was no way out, and Luca knew it. The smoke and dust momentarily cleared, and he saw them for what they were – just a bunch of frightened kids, trapped in a doomed building. They were going to die. They were all going to be crushed inside this awful, dark, burning thing, and there wasn't anything they could do about it.

We've completely failed, he thought. Did we really believe we would succeed? Did we fool ourselves so much that we could stop all of this?

Four figures stumbled out of the smoke, right next to him. It was Madoc and Gabriel, followed by Shorty and Tallboy. They looked more like ghosts than people, covered in dust and soot. A thick blob of blood had congealed above one of Shorty's eyes and he didn't look as if he would go much further. Tallboy was dragging him along. The scar-faced thug's constant smile was long gone. Now, he was just scared, like the rest of them. Even Gabriel had lost his usual calm silent menace. His mouth opened and closed, his hands were held up to protect his head.

Madoc stopped. Luca could have reached out and touched him, he was so close. They stood like that, like boxers who had nothing left to give, their hands by their sides, heads slumped to one side.

'You've lost, Broom,' Madoc croaked. 'The Black Prince has gone. I took the Devil's blood. I'm the king now. I'm the Pendragon. I'm the Pendragon!'

Madoc's ranting ignited something in Luca. He raged against the insanity of it all, the anger exploding from deep within. His vision blurred, then changed, darkening into black and whites. He shouted and screamed and roared, and the roar was all consuming. He dived at Madoc, hands raking at the man's chest, but they weren't hands any more – they were paws, with long claws. And he was towering over Madoc, glaring down at him, lashing out with blind uncontrollable fury, even as stones bounced off him and flames licked at his fur, and the transformation from boy to lion was complete.

Madoc was on the floor. The lion towered over him. Thick ropes of saliva dripped down onto Madoc's hair and face. The man tried to wipe it away but it was impossible. The lion leaned in, growling and grunting. He sniffed the air, sniffed his prey, could smell and taste the fear and the blood beating through the man's arteries. He opened his jaws, ready to bite.

A huge shock wave sent another load of masonry tumbling down. The lion was knocked to one side, momentarily stunned. Madoc screamed and scrabbled away, looking for anywhere to hide. The lion grabbed his ankle and dragged him back. Other voices were shouting around him, calling out Luca's name, begging him to stop, but the lion couldn't recognise the words. The rage was all-consuming. Nothing would stop him from killing this man.

Then a black blur raced out of the dense smoke and slammed into the lion's chest. He reeled back, off balance, roaring with rage and frustration, claws swiping at thin air. He was hit again, this time on the back of the head. He had no way of fending off the attack. Madoc was up on his feet and running. He disappeared into the smoke, followed by Gabriel and Tallboy, Shorty an unconscious lump across his shoulders. The lion started after them but another hit forced him back.

The lion was tiring, and the rage was dying, and as it did the first stirrings of awareness crept back into his brain. He roared, but it was more like a shout, and he swung his claws, but they were suddenly gone. The fur melted away. Luca slumped down. His head hurt where he had been hit. His eyes were stinging. He felt like he had been turned inside out.

It was Bran, of course, and a handful of surviving ravens, their feathers charred and damaged, some bleeding heavily and hardly able to fly. Bran landed next to him. The raven's wings stroked Luca's face. He tugged on Luca's ear. He chattered at him, pulling him this way and that.

'You should have let me kill him,' Luca groaned.

'No, he should not.'

It was Ambrose, emerging through the chaos, bathed in strange light, tall and thin, his face contorted with pain and grief.

'You?' raged Luca. 'Where have you been? Why don't you ever really help us?'

'I asked too much of you all. I should never have sent you here. I'm so sorry.'

'Freddie's dead! The Black Prince has done this, and Madoc got the Devil's blood anyway!'

'I know, and I have no words to explain how sorry I am. All I can do now is save the rest of you.'

Ambrose put his hands on Luca's shoulders. The roar of the chaos dimmed. A pale shimmering bubble spread out around all of them. Bran seemed almost hypnotised by it. The raven lay down on his belly, wings stretched out, beak partially open.

'You're safe in here,' Ambrose continued. 'Now listen. If you do as I say, Freddie may be the only one of you to die.'

'You make it sound like nothing,' Carter snarled. 'You're a bad as Madoc, old man.'

'Am I? You're wrong. I've watched too many knights die to want to ever see it again. My heart breaks for him. For Jess. For all of you.'

The bubble shimmered and faded and for a second Luca felt the heat of the fires. The noise level grew. Then Ambrose closed his eyes, concentrating. The bubble strengthened.

'We lost the swords,' Luca said, too exhausted to argue any more. 'They didn't work, anyway. My mum and McKenna are gone. It's all a total mess.'

'You forgot everything, son. You let fear and hate take over. That's why the swords stayed cold. They're not separate from you. They are an extension of you. Whatever you are, they are too.'

'So it's all over. Madoc's got away. The cathedral's collapsing. The Black Prince has cursed everything. And Freddie's dead.'

'For now, it does seem bleak, but I can save you, if you let me.'

They gathered around. Their faces were black with soot. They were filthy, cut and bruised, their clothes torn. They had no strength left. They couldn't go on. Luca stared into Jess's eyes. There was so much pain there. He wanted to hold her forever, to make it all better, to bring Freddie back.

'I know,' she said, reaching towards him. 'And I'm glad you didn't kill Madoc. You promised your mum, remember? Back at your flat, when you nearly changed. She would be proud of you.'

'I'm going to find her,' he said. 'That's my next promise.'

'And we'll all help you.'

'How can you be so strong?'

'I'm not really,' she said, sadly. 'Inside, part of me has died, but I want to live, Luca. I want us all to live. So let's do as Ambrose says.'

Ambrose smiled at her, and took her hand.

'Your brother did an incredibly brave thing.'

Jess nodded just once, then she wrapped Luca up in a hug.

'I can't lose you as well.'

Luca stood there, unable to move, his brain a kaleidoscope of thoughts and memories. All of the anger was gone. There was just sadness, and love, and an instinctive need to survive.

'Take my hands,' Ambrose said.

They moved together, and the bubble spread out further. The air was cool and fresh.

'Hold each other. Walk.'

Ambrose's voice was strained. He grimaced and closed his eyes. Sweat broke out across his forehead. They drifted through the ruins of the dying cathedral. Masonry bounced off the bubble and flames roared around them, but they safe inside. Ambrose gripped Luca's hand so tightly, he thought his fingers would break. He tried to let go, but Ambrose gripped him even harder.

'Just...hold on...keep walking...believing...walking...'

Luca suddenly understood. Ambrose wasn't just protecting them from the blows and the heat. He was absorbing it all himself. Another stone hit the bubble and Ambrose shuddered. They edged past a roaring fire. Red blotches welled across Ambrose's face.

'No,' Luca said. 'You can't take much more of this. Let go. We'll make it.'

'You won't.'

The effort of speaking was almost too much. Ambrose sagged at the knees and they lifted him up between them, and they carried on through the chaos. It seemed to go on for hours before they found a way to a jagged gash in the thick wall. They were outside. The bubble faded. Cold air rushed over them. Sleet soaked them, washing away the dirt and dust and blood.

'Run,' said Ambrose.

Then he collapsed onto the wet soil. Before Luca could reply, Ambrose faded away as if he never been there at all. One final, terrible aching roar came from the cathedral, and high above them the towers began to fall.

They ran.

36

Ambrose hadn't cried for more than a thousand years but now the tears poured. He gulped and sobbed. His shoulders heaved with the physical pain of what he was seeing. The dust cloud from the collapsed cathedral was more like a snow storm. He knew what was happening, and the sheer horror of it was too much even for him.

'I never believed...never imagined they wouldn't succeed...my fault...all my fault...'

His broken voice echoed around the impossible place where his broken body hovered between somewhere and nowhere, invisible to the children who were running away. He couldn't help them any more. He was no longer solid enough. The magic was gone. He would need to rest and recover and he would change again soon. Ambrose's time was nearly over.

Bran was suddenly next to him, breaking through from what was left of reality, and Ambrose stared at the raven as if he had no idea who or what he was. Bran pecked his fingers, pulling him towards a pale rectangle of light and possible escape from the madness. Ambrose allowed himself to be led. He moved like a cripple, staggering forwards on heavy feet, back bent, head down. The tears cut dark rivers through the dust on his face. His eyes were red raw and wild. Bran pulled and pulled, scratching and screaming.

Around them, the cathedral ruins and the whole of Canterbury melted away, to be replaced by a massive ugly castle with hundreds of narrow slits for windows and black flags hanging sullenly from the thick forbidding walls, and a confusing maze of muddy streets and densely packed thatched buildings leading in every direction.

'It's actually happened,' moaned Ambrose.

The smoke from a thousand cooking fires hung over everything. Chickens scattered away as he walked, and a mangy dog snarled hungrily at Bran. The sound of countless voices merged together with barking, shouting, screaming, singing, laughing, crying...all the noises of humans and animals living together in filthy squalor. The smell was appalling, a foul mix of sewer and rubbish dump.

The dog snapped at Bran twice more, and the raven flew up to get away, landing on the dirty straw roof of an alehouse. Ambrose stared in through the door. It was full of drunk men, fighting and singing. Some had already passed out. Those still standing ignored them. If they were in the way, they were trodden on like lumpy living rugs. It was a hellish scene.

'His curse has come true.'

A one-eyed man turned to see who had spoken. He grinned, revealing one black tooth. His face was covered in boils and sores. He scratched an armpit, checking to see what he might have dislodged, then he sucked at his fingernail with a noisy slurp.

'Who you cursing, stranger?'

Ambrose paused. He had to get a grip of the situation, in spite of the grief.

'Not you, my friend. I wish you nothing but great riches and a pretty wife. Tell me, if you will, what town is this?'

'What town?' the man repeated, as if the question was the most stupid thing he had ever heard. Ambrose nodded, happy to play the part of simpleton. He needed information, and quickly.

'Canterbury, you idiot. How many more towns are there around here?'

'Of course. I should have known. And the year? I'm afraid I've not been well. My mind tends to wander.'

The man cackled horribly. His breath stank of rotten cabbage and dead meat.

'Thirteen hundred and seventy six, so it is. The first year of the reign of our new and glorious king John the Second, he who was the Lord Madoc.'

The man bowed deeply, but he was too drunk to manage the manoeuvre without toppling over into the straw and mud that passed for a floor. Ambrose backed out of the alehouse. He had heard enough. He had to find Luca. He had to find them all.

'Bran,' he called, the grief replaced by silent fear and cold anger at what had been unleashed, 'Take to the air. See if you can spot any of them. Call in your brothers and sisters. Quickly, my friend.'

He kept his voice low, not wanting to attract any more attention from the thronging crowds, but nobody looked at him. They were too busy haggling over scraps of food or downing their bottles of toxic brew. Ambrose looked back at the castle. The wind had picked up a little and the flags were shifting in the breeze. He saw that they weren't plain black. Each flag had a circle painted on it, with thirteen segments, and in the top most segment a rough likeness of Madoc sneered down at him. The insanity of it was overwhelming. In an instant, hundreds of years of history wiped out, replaced by this abomination, this alternative primitive medieval world where Madoc was king. And where the children were in grave danger, it they hadn't already been captured or worse.

He headed out of the town, past the swinging bodies of thieves and bandits, past the great dumps of rubbish, past the clogged slime of what once must have been a fast flowing river but was now nothing but a green ditch full of anything the people felt like throwing into it. Ambrose shook his head. The magic that had created this hell was darker than anything he had ever seen in all his years. At that moment, he had absolutely no idea how things could ever be put right.

He stopped in a small clump of trees around a mile from the town walls. He rested there, waiting for Bran. Darkness had fallen by the time the raven returned. He was alone.

'Any sign?'

Bran screamed and chattered, shaking his huge head from side to side.

'Then we keep searching. They're out there, Bran. I have to find them. And I have to find a way to break this spell.'

A deep frost was forming. The air crackled with it. Ambrose looked down at his hands. They were changing. He tried to hold on to the memory of this body but it was no good. When he woke next, he would be someone new entirely. Only the tattoos on his arm would help him remember any of it all. Bran pressed against him, desperate to help in any way he could, but it was hopeless. The frost thickened around Ambrose's lifeless body and hours passed in silence. Then at some point in the freezing night, the frost was melted away in a sudden flare of light.

Merlin's new form stood up. Bran eyed the newcomer warily, unsure what to make of it.

'It's still me,' the young girl said, holding out her arm for Bran to see. 'And now our search begins.'

ACKNOWLEDGEMENTS

Writing a book is never a solitary venture. Thanks go to:

Amy Keogh at SpringSignal - for fine website design and advice. Ed Bettison – what a wonderful artist you are. The many school teachers and librarians who have been incredibly supportive and enthusiastic about this whole project. Madeleine & George – for just rolling your eyes and bringing me back down to earth in the way that children should. Freya Tebbutt – thanks for lending me your name. Nick & Tania Smith – for always being so enthusiastic about this project. Dianne & Barry Haskey – for continued support and interest. Damian & Amanda Scally – for long chats, lots of laughs and red wine. Jo & Barry Smith – for friendship and support beyond measure. The Tebbutts, McKennas and Quartleys - best bunch of mates in the world. Finally, Sara – thank you for coming along with me on this crazy journey and enjoying it as much as I do. You are incredible. We seize every day.

Finian Black

.

Finian Black

Made in the USA
Columbia, SC
23 September 2018